Will
The Ingram Brothers #1

By
Roz Lee

Will
Ingram Brothers #1
Copyright © 2019 Roz Lee
Published by State of Mind
ISBN: 978-1-7327839-5-9 (eBook)
978-1-7327839-4-2 (Paperback)

This eBook is a work of fiction. Any names, characters, places, and events portrayed in this work are products of the author's imagination or are used fictitiously. Any resemblance to actual events, places or persons, living or dead, is coincidental. No part of this eBook may be used or reproduced in any form whatsoever in any country whatsoever without the express written permission of the authors, except in the case of brief quotations embodied in reviews.

Author's Note

Thank you so much for purchasing *Will – The Ingram Brothers #1*. If the town of Willowbrook, Texas and some of the characters seem familiar, then I'll assume you've also read *Lost Melody* by my alter ego, Dolores W. Maroney. If you haven't, then Melody, Hank, and a few other characters will be new to you. No worries. I loved the town of Willowbrook and its residents so much I had to go back there to see what they were up to. I hope you'll love them as much as I do, and if you haven't read *Lost Melody*, will choose do so when you've finished reading Will's story.

In the meantime, I'm working on Jake's story with Rick's following along soon.

Thanks again. I hope you enjoy the read.

Roz

CHAPTER ONE

William Ingram stared at the drink he held loosely between his thumb and middle finger. Was this going to be his only drink today or the first of many? In the last six months, he'd gone from mildly successful to virtually broke. So, the decision was a no-brainer. It would be the first of many—or at least the first of as many as he could afford.

The boarding pass in his jacket pocket and the drink in front of him represented the majority of the funds he had left to his name. The few art supplies he hadn't sold at rock-bottom prices to fund his return home had been checked as luggage which, an airline employee by the name of Brandy had assured him, would be transferred to the new plane as soon it arrived to take him and the rest of the passengers aboard their aborted flight on to their destination.

Just his luck. He'd admitted defeat and then his flight from New York made an emergency landing in Philadelphia. It seemed the universe wasn't done with him.

The airline had booked as many of the stranded passengers onto existing flights as possible, starting with the ones who were making a connection in Dallas. He wished he was one of them, but the truth was, once he got to Texas, he was there to stay. He'd ventured out into the world, had followed his dream until it had turned into a nightmare. When things had gone to shit, he'd raged and fought back, convinced the police would eventually find the people responsible and return his property to him. After several months with no break in the case, his confidence had eroded until he'd lost hope and slid down the slippery slope into despair. His girlfriend/agent had stolen more than his livelihood, she'd stolen his will to create, leaving him one option—cut his losses and return home to Willowbrook, Texas.

What he'd do once he got there was anyone's guess. Maybe he could get a job painting houses. It was honest work and required the one thing he still had—an able body. He'd never been one to do much physical labor, avoiding it at all costs, but in New York, he'd seen the necessity of keeping in shape and had been a regular at the local gym until he'd had to cancel his membership due to lack of funds. He'd never painted a structure before, but he knew how to hold a paintbrush. It wasn't like anyone would be asking his opinion on the color or anything else. He'd be hired muscle to get the mindless job done.

He gave himself two, maybe three weeks before the mind-numbing physical exertion pushed him to the edge of his sanity.

Great. Just fucking great.

He took a healthy sip, closing his eyes as the cheap bourbon ate away at the lining of his throat and nibbled at the ragged edges of his mood.

A knee to his hip almost knocked him off his seat and caused the liquor in his glass to slosh over the side onto the back of his hand. Grabbing the bar to steady himself, he groaned at the waste of alcohol he'd been counting on. "Shit! Watch what you're doing!"

"Sorry."

The feminine voice slid through him like fifty-year-old whiskey, setting fire to parts of him that had suffered Jessica's betrayal perhaps more than any other. It was good to know the physical damage wasn't permanent even if he had no intention of taking any part of himself out for a test run. Determined not to engage, he sucked the liquid from his skin. The bartender hustled over with a rag, drawing Will's attention upward. His gaze locked on the reflection in the mirror behind the bar, and he damn near bit his hand as he recognized the woman sitting next to him.

He didn't know her name, but he'd seen her before. More importantly, he'd seen her type before. Beautiful, sexy, and high-maintenance. Everything from her clothes to her hairstyle to the perfect application of makeup on her clear complexion screamed *rich girl.*

She'd been on his flight—in first class while he'd been lucky to be in the cheap seats. If not for the cute flight attendant who'd taken pity on him and offered to let him change seats, free of charge, to an open bulkhead seat, he never would have seen this woman. She'd come breezing in at the last minute like she owned the plane, and taken her seat next to the aisle in the last row. Just feet from where he sat trying not to notice anything about her. Of course he'd noticed everything, from the color of her hair—auburn—to the shape of her body—a perfect hourglass—to the slight sheen of perspiration on her forehead as she shoved her Louis Vuitton carry-on into the overhead bin. He'd looked her over as a man then and liked what he saw, but now, with only her face visible in the mirror, the artist in him took over.

She wore makeup, but it was artfully applied, so, at first glance, it appeared she wore none at all. Strategically placed streaks of—whatever-the-hell-women-called-it—highlighted already distinct cheekbones. Some sort of dark magic applied to her eyelids showcased the most beautiful blue irises he'd ever seen. Shades of blue paint swirled through his mind as his brain automatically tried to replicate the color in his preferred medium—oils.

Coupling what he'd already seen of her body with what he now knew about her face, he realized he had to paint her. Only he didn't paint anymore. The sharpness of the realization had him reaching for the glass the bartender had so kindly refilled at no cost. Forcing his gaze from the mirror, Will gulped the last of his whiskey. Placing the cheap highball glass on the bar, he contemplated his next move. He couldn't paint her, but there was something else he could do to her, and he wanted to do the *something else* even more than he wanted to commit her likeness to canvas. Just because he'd sworn off relationships didn't register in his thinking. This was a one-time deal. Nothing more. They were two passengers on a one-way trip to Hell. Well, that was *his* story, but they were passengers on the same cursed flight. What would a little fuck between strangers hurt?

The barkeep arrived with the woman's order, and Will signaled for a refill of his own. He'd expected to see something pink with an umbrella or maybe a cutesy martini glass rimmed with sugar and swirled with chocolate sauce. Instead, her drink looked suspiciously like his. No-nonsense. No ice. Just two fingers of amber liquid—probably the good stuff. She surprised him by knocking the contents back with one swallow. She didn't even gasp for air afterward, confirming his suspicions about the quality of the whiskey. It was either good whiskey or there was more to her than he'd thought.

He couldn't wait to find out. He turned to face her. "Hi. Looks like we're going to be here for a while. Know someplace we can go to kill some time?"

"That's the worst pickup line I've ever heard." And MacKenzie had heard plenty. However, none had tempted her the way this one had from the Hot Guy she'd spied earlier in the boarding area at JFK. Tall, dark, and handsome despite his grim countenance. And despite her recent vow to abstain from anything with a Y chromosome, his voice ignited something inside her she'd almost hoped was dead for good. Men were trouble. It was a lesson well learned from her latest failed relationship. Men thought with their little head more often than not, and it tended to lead them astray.

Like the guy on the barstool next to her.

Yes, after determining she wasn't going anywhere anytime soon, she'd made a quick stop at the ladies' room then gone in search of him. He'd been easy to find. Their gate was at the far end of the terminal, and he'd stopped at the first bar he'd run across.

She couldn't blame him. She needed a drink in the worst way possible, as clearly did he. Travel could tempt a person to drink, especially when things went awry, as they had today. She didn't know anything about how planes worked, but she figured if the pilot decided he needed to set the thing down as quickly as possible, then whatever had gone wrong must have been major. The way she saw it, she was lucky to be alive, even if her life was a shit-storm.

If today's events didn't call for a couple of fingers of Macallan and a good fuck to celebrate surviving a near-death experience, then nothing did. She'd save the recriminations for later—like when she got to Texas and started her new job. From what she'd heard of the small town where she'd be living, she'd have plenty of time to visit past regrets and beat herself up over her poor decisions in regard to men. It didn't appear there was anything else to do there.

Her savings were dwindling fast. Thankfully, her new employer had sprung for the plane ticket—first class—much to her surprise, leaving the remains of her nest egg untouched. She'd need most of it to get settled. She had no idea what a place rented for in off-the-grid Texas, but she assumed it was considerably less than what it would have cost her to rent a place of her own in Manhattan. After her boyfriend/boss had gone missing, she'd had no choice but to move out of his modern high-rise and into a friend's closet. It hadn't actually been a closet, but Bethany had been using it as one and probably was again since MacKenzie had cleared out.

She'd calculated and recalculated her financial situation enough times the grim figures were etched on her brain. Pocket change was short, but she still had room on her American Express card. With a bit of luck, she'd be able to pay it down once she was receiving regular paychecks again.

The guy sitting next to her didn't need to know her hard-luck story. Today was about celebrating life and maybe just a little about celebrating her *new* life, and that was on her. Today, she wasn't the loser who'd been duped and dumped. Today, she was a strong woman with a future. A woman who saw what she wanted and went after it.

And she wanted...him.

She dug the well-worn card from her wallet and waved it at the bartender. He hustled over. Making a sweeping motion with her hand to indicate Hot Guy's drink and hers, she said, "Close out our tabs, please."

Hot Guy's head jerked up. "I can pay my own way."

"I'm sure you can, but allow me." Before he could argue further, she thrust her card at the bartender who snatched it like it was platinum instead of green plastic, smirked at Hot Guy then took off to process the sale.

"No, really," Hot Guy protested.

MacKenzie signaled him to stop. Fantasy was about all she had left and she'd be damned if he was going to ruin this one. "I've got it." She slid off the stool, deliberately letting her breasts brush his arm. The bartender returned with the charge slip which she signed and slid back to him. Grabbing the extended handle on her carry-on, she made eye contact with Hot Guy. "You coming? Or not?"

It was all she could do not to look over her shoulder to see if he followed her. Once she'd made it out to the crowded concourse, he caught up to her. "Where are we going?"

"Someplace private."

He said nothing, just matched his stride to hers and used his broad shoulders to clear a path for her. If she hadn't been as nervous as a cat in a room full of rocking chairs, she would have admired the little bit of chivalry from a man who didn't have a clue where they were headed. Now, if she could only remember where the article she'd read in the magazine she'd found in the seat-back pocket had said the micro suites were located. She hadn't paid much attention since she'd never in a million years envisioned being in a situation where she'd actually use one. She'd been impressed at the number of airports where the mini-hotels had been installed and wondered if they'd been selected because they had the highest number of stranded passengers, or if there'd been another reason. What did it matter? She was horny and they had one here—somewhere. She scanned the directional signs posted overhead for a hint then, there it was! On the wall, sandwiched between the ladies' room and an automated candy dispenser hung a giant illuminated advertisement for the fancy no-tell motel. Noting the location, she made a quick assessment of their whereabouts then pointed. "That way. It isn't far now." She hoped.

A right turn sent them down another wide concourse lined with stores selling souvenirs and survival gear for weary travelers. Nestled in their midst was an oasis of calm. MacKenzie stopped. The check-in desk reminded her of a mid-range hotel chain with its faux wood counter and cheap artwork.

"Whoa. Wait a minute."

She whipped her head around to glare at Hot Guy. "What? You've changed your mind?"

His head swiveled from side to side. "No. I haven't changed my mind, but I was thinking of something a little less expensive—like a janitor's closet or something."

"I'm going to pretend you didn't just say that and get us a room. Will an hour be enough?"

"Sure."

"Wait here. I'll be right back." The disinterested employee behind the counter walked her through the check-in process with all the enthusiasm of a turnip. Under other circumstances, she'd be annoyed, but none of it mattered in this instance. She held the key up for Hot Guy to see then, heart pounding, she strode past the desk to the short hall, dragging her carry-on behind.

She waved the keycard in front of the electronic lock mechanism and clasped the telescopic handle on her suitcase. "Allow me." Hot Guy's body pressed against her from behind. A long arm reached around her to push and hold the door open for her. It wasn't much, another one of those chivalrous acts she'd grown unaccustomed to in New York, but it did unexpected things to her insides.

"Thank...thank you," she said as she stumbled over the threshold, the sight of his hand, purely masculine, with long fingers and strong knuckles making her clumsy, and for the first time since she'd decided to take him up on his offer, nervous. *What the hell am I doing?* She didn't know this guy from Adam. He could be a serial killer or...or...something. But damn, he smelled good—like the Catskills on a warm summer day. If he'd been a tree, she'd hug the shit out of him.

The door swooshed shut, the sound of a dead bolt sliding into place sounding like the final nail in her coffin. Whirling around, she gasped at the sight of him leaning against the door, his arms behind his back and his ankles crossed. His eyes blazed with a heat she'd only read about in romance novels as he slowly undressed her with his gaze. The tiniest hint of a smile as he completed his inspection told her how much he liked what he'd seen. Turnabout was fair play. She released her tight grip on her luggage then kicked off her shoes before returning the favor.

Her first impression of him at JFK was that he was a man who took care of himself, and, at closer inspection, she'd been right. She'd bet the available balance on her last credit card there was a sculpted body beneath his expensively cut suit coat and tailored dress shirt. His tight-fitting jeans, worn nearly white in all the right places, left little to the imagination. She checked him out all the way down to the Italian leather loafers on his feet before letting her gaze slide up again to caress what promised to be a very generous package barely contained behind a button fly. Whoever he was, he had style. In fact, he reminded her of a guy she'd seen on the cover of a magazine once. She'd gotten herself off to the cover, and, after the magazine had gone missing, to the memory of it, more times than she dared recall.

Finished with her perusal, she dragged her eyes back up to his.

"Thanks for getting us a room, but you don't have to do this."

And he's too fucking nice. She didn't want nice. She wanted wild-monkey sex. The kind where words weren't necessary. Where both parties took what they wanted without regard to the needs of the other. There was only one thing she wanted to know. "Do you have protection?"

"I do." The timbre of his voice nearly melted her panties off.

MacKenzie dipped her chin once to acknowledge his answer then reached for the top button on her blouse.

CHAPTER TWO

*H**oly, fuckin' shit.*
Will could hardly believe his eyes. Maybe his luck was changing. How else could he explain the goddess doing a striptease before him?

Maybe she was a siren sent by the Fates to finish him off. If so, she was doing an excellent job of incinerating him. Fists clenched behind him, he forced himself to remain glued to the door as she slowly revealed herself to him, one inch of creamy skin at a time.

Like any piece of exquisite art, she deserved to be admired, to be studied, and knowing this would be his one and only chance to do so, he took in the sight before him with both his artist's vision and the appreciation of a human male who had seen his fair share of nude females.

He'd recognized her beauty from the beginning, but even his artist's eye couldn't have imagined the gentle swell of her breasts or the sweet curve of her hips or, god help him, the enticing pillow of a belly that drove him insane with lust. That part of the female anatomy seemed so womanly to him. He was glad to see she hadn't tried to diet it away like most women did these days.

As a teenager, he'd fallen in love with the paintings of voluptuous nudes by the old masters. While his brothers and friends had studied purloined centerfolds, he'd studied Rubens and Bouguereau. A woman's body was a thing of beauty to be admired and, in this instance, coveted. Any man would be fortunate if they could claim her as theirs, but it wasn't in the cards for him. He had this one opportunity, and, as much as his fingers itched for a piece of charcoal and a pad of paper, he needed the physical release more—needed this reminder he was still alive.

Mustering as much restraint as he could, he lifted his right hand and, with his index finger, signaled for her to turn around. Her lips curved into a seductive smile then she did a graceful about-face, peeking over her shoulder to gauge his reaction which was immediate. Will pushed away from the door with one thing on his mind, taking what she so freely offered.

Fully clothed, he pressed his front to her back. The need to touch her, to commit every inch of her body to tactile memory was almost more than he could bear, but to touch her the way he wanted to would make this encounter too personal. There was nothing personal about it. She wanted to be fucked, and by god, he wanted to oblige her. No names. No more physical contact than was absolutely necessary to get the job done. An anonymous encounter they'd both, hopefully, recall fondly years from now. Hell, if it went no further, he'd be eternally grateful to this woman, though she'd never know what she'd done for him. He hadn't looked forward to anything in months.

Hoping he didn't need words to get his message across, he nestled the hard ridge of his erection in the cleft of her cheeks and, with a subtle nudge of his hips, silently demanded she move closer to the sofa. God bless her, she took the hint and shuffled her feet in the right direction.

"Stop," he growled in her ear. "Bend over."

She bent at the waist and braced herself on the edge of the pleather sleeper/sofa. A tap with his foot against hers and she spread her legs, offering her priceless treasure for him to plunder.

Will removed his wallet, extracted his in-case-of-an-emergency condom, clenched the packet between his teeth then returned his wallet to his pocket. There was precious little in the billfold, but he couldn't afford to leave it behind, and god knew if he'd have any brain cells left when he was done. Better to pack it away now.

Valuables stowed, he slipped the top button on his fly through the well-worn buttonhole with ease. Then he did the next one and the next. He didn't bother with the last one. Hooking his thumbs in the waistband, he shoved the denim until it bunched at his hips. From there, it was a simple thing to maneuver the front of his briefs out of the way.

Shit. He nearly came at the sight of his dick, engorged and throbbing, laying heavy on the curve of her creamy smooth backside. He was fucking ready, but was she? He'd always been careful to make sure his partner was prepared, and had just enough courtesy left in him to do the same for her. A two-finger swipe between her legs brought a groan to both their lips. He'd never donned a raincoat as fast as he did then.

Positioning the head of his cock at her entrance, with the last vestiges of his control, he growled out, "Tell me to stop now or hold the fuck on."

Spontaneous. Human. Combustion. The words crystallized in her brain. Pseudo-scientific bullshit—or so she'd thought up until this moment. Naked and spread wide, waiting for this stranger to fuck her senseless, she was perilously close to going up in flames. He hadn't removed a stitch of clothing, and god, wasn't that hot? No sweet talk unless she considered his warning to *hold the fuck on* sweet, but damn if her insides hadn't turned to liquid at his gruff command. She'd never done anything like this in her life and had to wonder why the fuck not as she gave him the consent he demanded. With a shift of her weight, she pushed her hips back and drove herself onto his cock.

Sweet mother of god.

He was thick and hard, and as he flexed his hips and filled her the rest of the way, her toes curled into the industrial-grade carpet, and her fingers instinctively dug into the upholstery. A groan of pure pleasure escaped her lips. He gripped her hips with hands so hot she was certain he'd branded her with his touch. He pulled all the way out of her then slammed back in. If not for him holding her, she would have collapsed from the force of his thrust.

This is what it feels like to be taken.

This wasn't love. It was pure lust unleashed without restraint, and she loved it.

She'd been desired before, but it had always been tempered with civility and/or consideration, but there had *always* been caution. There was no caution here. Hot Guy took her as if he owned her. Like it was his right, and only his, to fuck her. And as he rode her like a cowboy on the run from the law, she thought for a moment, it wasn't an illusion. He was running from something and he was taking her with him.

I'm his. No one will ever do it for me the way he does. It was a crazy thought, driven from her mind as his balls slapped an age-old rhythm against her clit, and the delicious pain of tender tissues stretching to take all of him coalesced into a dizzying need to come.

As if he'd read her body, he tightened his hold on her hips and said the magic words. "Take it, baby. Suck me dry."

Dear. God.

His words were filthy and raunchy and the sexiest thing she'd ever heard. The image they created in her brain, of bringing this powerful man to his knees, was all it took. The tremors began in her thighs and spread upward where they detonated charges in her womb. Her clit throbbed; her nipples tingled. When her pussy spasmed around the steel pole reaming her, Hot Guy let out a primal groan and lost control. His thrusts became short. His groin ground against her as if he was trying to burrow deep inside her and never come out, and, in some way, he had. With a string of profanities directed at a supreme being, he came, filling the tip of the condom with scalding cum.

The moment he let go of her, MacKenzie's knees gave out and she tumbled face-first onto the sofa bed. Breathless and feeling like a rag doll, she must look a sight, but she couldn't find it within herself to care. She'd move—eventually—then she'd thank Hot Guy. Maybe offer to buy him another drink. It was the least she could do for his stellar performance. She hadn't been with many men, but she'd been with enough to know what she'd felt, what she'd experienced today was beyond compare. Hot Guy was a sex god, and he had the equipment to match his status. It was a shame they'd never see each other again. She could get used to his style of sex on a regular basis.

The sound of the door opening spurred MacKenzie to action. Bolting upright, she crossed her arms over her breasts and winced as the pleather upholstery snagged her bare ass as she tried to scoot into a sitting position. By the time she peeled her abused flesh off the sofa and resettled, she opened her mouth. "Wait!" hovered in the air, a second too late as the door closed. Hot Guy was gone.

"Asshole." MacKenzie tucked an errant strand of hair behind her ear. Maybe he'd just gone out to get something from the vending machine. She could use a snack herself. Glancing around the room, her gaze fell on the small desk on the opposite wall. The keycard she'd used to open the door lay right where she'd dropped it when they first entered. Her lungs deflated as she spied the used condom lying like a testament to her folly in the bottom of the waste basket. Hot Guy, aka Asshole, wasn't coming back.

Gathering her clothes, she dressed then curled her legs beneath her on the sofa. She'd paid for an hour, might as well take advantage of the privacy to get her head on straight. She didn't think her lady parts were going to stop humming a satisfied tune anytime soon, but she could hope. There was a good chance she'd see Hot Guy again at the gate and she didn't want him to see how his abrupt departure had affected her. Would it have killed him to hang around another minute, perhaps inquire as to her well-being?

He's a love 'em and leave 'em—no—a fuck 'em and flee type.

"What did you expect?" she mumbled to herself. "You picked him up in an airport bar for cryin' out loud." If the situation didn't have pathetic loser written all over it, she didn't know what did. The biggest problem was, she didn't know which of them the label applied to. Her for encouraging Hot Guy or him for taking her up on the offer. It could go either way, but no doubt about it, he was an asshole. If she never saw him again, it would be too soon.

CHAPTER THREE

"Thanks for coming to get me." Will embraced his older brother, Jake, in the baggage claim area.

"We couldn't let you hitchhike to Willowbrook," his younger brother, Rick, said as he engulfed William in a tight hug. His brother felt solid, more like the soldier he'd been, up until the war on terrorism had chewed him up and spit him out nearly a year ago. Over Rick's shoulder, Will's gaze locked with Jake's. The brothers shared a meaningful look. Now was not the time for them to discuss Rick's recovery or his future. There'd be plenty of time to dissect each other's lives once they were all home. "Glad you're back, bro."

"Thanks." He just wished his homecoming was under different circumstances, but like Rick, only a catastrophe could have convinced him to return to Willowbrook for anything more than a visit. Unless pigs sprouted wings, he was here to stay. He wasn't so sure about Rick. Something else they needed to talk about.

"Would you look at that," Jake murmured. William turned to see what had caught his brother's attention.

After he left her, he'd tucked his balled fists into his pockets and walked until he'd found what was possibly the only deserted place in the terminal and leaned against the wall to catch his breath. Only then did he bring the fingers he'd swiped through her juices up to his nose. Inhaling deep, he let her scent take him back to their rented room, to the woman he'd never forget.

It had taken some work on his part, but he'd managed to avoid seeing her in the Philadelphia airport until they'd called his flight. He'd boarded earlier than most and been satisfied with his seat as far from first class as possible. Heck, he didn't know for certain they'd been on the same plane. She could have been waiting on a connecting flight to anywhere for all he knew. They'd exchanged orgasms, not itineraries. But there she was, on the other side of the baggage carousel, a shit-ton of expensive luggage piled on a cart being pushed by a man in the livery of a chauffeur. He hated the way his body responded to her presence. He'd taken what she offered, thinking it would be more than enough, but as the plane had made its way across the country, he'd been surprised to find out it hadn't been nearly enough. Her orgasm had done something to him he couldn't name then she'd collapsed onto the sofa, and he'd had visions of her sprawled across a velvet chaise, looking like she'd just been fucked. He'd wanted to put a just-fucked expression on her face then paint her more than he'd wanted his next breath. He'd had no choice but to leave.

"Seeing *her* is worth the trip, Billy boy."

Will cringed at Jake's use of the nickname he hated with a passion.

"Hey, is that yours?" Rick pointed to a beat-up cardboard box coming around the bend in the carousel. It appeared a band of gorillas had ripped it apart then patched it back together with tape bearing the TSA logo.

"Yeah." Will stepped toward the luggage conveyor, but Rick's hand on his shoulder stopped him.

"I'll get it."

He opened his mouth to protest, but Jake's elbow dug into his ribs. "Let him. He seems to feel a need to be useful these days."

A lump the size of Texas formed in Will's throat. He nodded, silently acknowledging what his brother was saying. Of the three of them, Rick had always been the one to offer a helping hand—thus his desire to enter the military. When he'd first come home, he wouldn't even help himself, much less someone else. He was glad to see this small indication his younger brother still lived inside the shell of a man who had returned to them. Maybe there was hope for Rick after all.

Rick joined them a few minutes later with the battered box tucked under one arm and the strap of Will's giant duffel slung over the opposite shoulder. "Is this everything?"

"Yeah." Not much to show for nearly a decade of life. He reached for the duffel.

Rick shrugged him off. "I've got it."

Jake fell into step beside Will as they followed their younger brother out into the Texas heat. As they crossed the busy roadway to the parking garage, Will caught himself scanning the people loading luggage into cars at the curb, wanting one last look at her—for posterity's sake, he told himself. It wasn't like he was ever going to see her again. He knew for a fact he didn't frequent the kinds of places she did. Everything about her screamed money and class—two things he most certainly didn't have and wouldn't find where he was going. The only thing they had in common was a shared air-travel experience and good sex. Hell, maybe the best sex he'd ever had, if he was being honest with himself. Best to put her out of his mind and get on with his life—whatever that was going to entail.

MacKenzie smiled at the driver who'd been sent to pick her up. She'd expected someone in a pickup truck, not a limo. From what she'd heard about her new employer, he didn't flaunt his wealth or celebrity status. By all accounts, he was a humble, yet incredibly talented man. She appreciated the first-class treatment while reminding herself not to get used to it. He was just trying to make her transition from New York to Texas easier. She couldn't expect to be pampered once she was settled. She doubted the small town where she'd be living had cab service, much less limo service. Besides, a car came with the job—something she'd need since her employer lived outside of town. He'd converted an old barn on his property into state-of-the-art workspace. She'd have an office there, but live in town.

She forced her brain to focus on reining in her expectations of the place instead of obsessing over Hot Guy. She'd managed to avoid him in the Philly airport, wasn't even certain they would be on the same flight to Dallas. He could have been waiting in the bar for a completely different flight. She hadn't asked, and he hadn't offered. What he had offered, she'd accepted way too easily. He'd given her what she wanted then sprinted out of there like the TSA was after him for a strip search.

She couldn't blame him. She'd been two seconds away from breaking her own hastily adopted airport hookup rules. Rule number one being—under no circumstances exchange personal information, i.e. name, phone number, destination—and god forbid—relationship status. Rule number two—under no circumstances beg him for a repeat. One and done. It was the only way.

Then she'd spied him at baggage claim. If not for Bernie? Bennie? *Her driver,* she might have hurdled the carousel like a crazed fan at a rock concert and broken all of her rules for the chance at one more time with him.

He'd seemed more relaxed than he'd been in Philly. Maybe it was the warm greeting from the sexy as hell guys who met him, or maybe he was happy to see his friends? Family? It was difficult to tell from across the carousel. They were all tall with dark hair. If they were related, they each had a distinctive style. The tallest one wore work boots, jeans, and a ragged T-shirt. She wouldn't be surprised to find out he could benchpress a horse. The idea gained momentum when he gathered Hot Guy's baggage, lifting the tattered box and duffel as if they weighed nothing. The other one was the polar opposite of Buff Guy. His suit branded him a professional of some kind—banker, lawyer, corporate exec. His attire fit him well, but she preferred the sexy, sophisticated style Hot Guy sported. There was something about a guy in jeans topped with a smart blazer that did it for her. Especially when she knew what those jeans held.

Perfection.

Yeah, it was a good thing the chauffeur found her when he did. He'd saved her from making a complete fool of herself. It was time to look forward, not back. Her mistakes were behind her, her future a blank slate waiting for her to write a new chapter. Pulling her attention away from the trio of sexy men, she counted the bags stacked on her cart, came up with the correct number, and waved the driver on. It took every bit of self-control she could muster to raise her chin and follow him out the door, without glancing over her shoulder.

"It's about an hour's drive, ma'am." The car pulled away from the curb and accelerated into traffic. "There's water in the mini-fridge on your left."

"Thanks—"

His gaze caught hers in the rearview mirror. There was a smile in his voice when he said, "Bernie, ma'am. No problem. You just relax. Leave the traffic worries to me."

It had been a long time since she'd met with such kindness. Courtesy wasn't a required trait for drivers in Manhattan. Mad driving skills were. If they got you there in one piece, they were good. If you also arrived on time, they were fabulous.

She thanked him again before he raised the glass partition sealing her into a cocoon of silence. God, it felt good to close her eyes and let the rhythm of the road lull her to sleep. She'd done nothing but run at full blast since she'd accepted the job offer in Texas. She'd pared her belongings down to the bare necessities, packed her bags, said goodbye to her friends and colleagues, promising to keep in touch. Her client had an apartment in New York City he co-owned with his partners. She'd been given the go-ahead to use it as needed whenever her new job dictated a trip to the Big Apple, which it occasionally would. He'd also mentioned his agent lived in the city. She'd be expected to work with him on certain projects, too. But her main job would be here, managing publicity for her new boss—Hank Travis.

How in heaven's name she'd ended up working for a rock star—scratch that—a superstar rock band, she'd never understand. She'd been a fan of BlackWing for as long as she could remember. Now, she was going to work for them! She'd been even more surprised to find out her friend Sunny Sheldon knew Hank and his wife, Melody. She'd called on her friends to get MacKenzie this job. The jury was still out on whether she could live in a small Texas town without losing her mind, but what choice did she have? After things had gone south with her previous job, she'd tapped everyone in the PR industry she knew and had come up with zip. Sunny had come through for her. She owed it to her friend to give this her best effort, even if it felt like she was being shipped off to another planet.

They'd left civilization behind almost the minute they departed the airport. MacKenzie gazed out the window at the passing scenery. Trees. Fields of...were those crops? God, she was in over her head. Visions of scruffy men in overalls and women in dowdy paisley dresses down to their ankles flashed across her brain. She was going to die out here in the wilderness. These...farmers probably ate people like her for lunch.

Maybe she could talk Hank into letting her work from home. She could rent a place in Dallas. Video conferencing was practically as good as talking in person. She could do her job remotely. She was certain of it.

The car slowed as they passed through a town. MacKenzie prayed it wasn't her destination. This was worse than she'd imagined. Empty storefronts. Weed-infested sidewalks. Pickup trucks with gun racks in the back window. She'd never survive in a place like this. She didn't relax until the driver turned a corner and she saw a sign indicating her new home was another twenty miles down the road.

Please. Please don't let it be the same. Please.

She remained on edge, surveying the vast empty spaces punctuated by the occasional house, some with barns, some without. When she spied the city limit sign declaring the population of her new home to just over two thousand, she had to hold back her tears. This was going to be awful. Two thousand people? That was...nothing!

"Welcome to Willowbrook, miss." The driver's voice made her sit up and take a deep breath. "Mr. Travis suggested I give you a short tour of the town before heading out to his place."

She couldn't imagine what Hank's reasoning was, but the more information she had about her situation, the better she'd be able to negotiate a move to Dallas. "Thank you, Bernie."

"My pleasure, miss. My mother grew up here. It's a nice place."

The affection in his voice eased the tightness in her shoulders just a little bit. Bernie drove slowly, stopping where it was convenient to give her a better look at a particular location. He pointed out several churches, the schools, the post office and municipal building then circled the park at one end of town. MacKenzie gasped at the heart of the town. Disney's Main Street had nothing on this one. The buildings were quaint and well maintained. The storefronts vibrant with sparkling glass to display their wares.

"Most people around here don't have much, but they take care of what they do have," Bernie said, taking a left off the busy downtown street. "This is my favorite part of town. All the streets are named for trees. Oak. Maple. Pecan. You get the idea. My grandmother lived on Walnut." He made another turn, and MacKenzie powered the window down to get a better view.

Air fragrant with the scent of fresh-cut grass rushed in. It was as different from Manhattan as a place could be, but as she filled her lungs, she thought perhaps it wouldn't be the worst place to live. She scanned the street. The houses were mostly post-war bungalows, painted white with various color shutters, but that was where the similarity ended. Yards were lovingly tended, planted with flowers and shrubs to match the owner's personality. And lining the street were the most magnificent old-growth trees she'd ever seen.

"It's beautiful."

"Yes, ma'am. It is. All the streets in this neighborhood are like this. If you're hunting for a place to live, this would be my choice. It's hard to get in though. Most of these people have owned their houses since they were built after World War II. They've been passed down to kids and grandkids. It's rare to see one go on the market."

"Guess I won't be living here, then," she said, powering the window up.

"Do you have a place?"

"My employer said they'd arranged something for me."

"I'm sure you'll like it." Bernie steered them back out onto Main Street then on to the outskirts of town. "We're almost there." He pointed out the window. "See the big barn with the wings painted on it?"

MacKenzie craned her neck to get a glimpse of her new place of employment. The giant barn rose up from the expanse of crops, its black wings making it stand out from the others she'd seen along the road. She swallowed hard, willing the nerves fluttering like a flock of ravens in her stomach to settle. *I can do this. I can do this.* So what if the job was in the middle of nowhere? A job was a job. BlackWing needed a PR guru, so here she was.

"WELCOME HOME," RICK said as they made the last turn and headed into Willowbrook. Will nodded and mentally added one to the tally displayed on the population sign marking the official boundary. "Lot of people gonna be glad to see you."

"Like who?" He'd never been particularly popular in school and hadn't wasted a minute longer than necessary leaving after graduation.

"Hank, for one," Jake offered. "I saw him the other day at the diner. He asked about you, and I told him you were moving back."

Will closed his eyes and took a deep breath, letting his frustration out with it. He'd been so caught up in his misery, he hadn't given much thought to what it would actually be like living here again. In the same graduating class, they'd known each other since they were in diapers. Hank had lived a few blocks down on the same street. They'd played together as toddlers and stuck beside each other as teenagers when their interests went beyond Friday night football. Hank had been into music and opted to lead the drumline in the high school band, while Will had contributed to the gridiron insanity by painting the team mascot on the paper banner the team demolished by running through it at the beginning of every game. To this day, he could draw a wildcat with his eyes closed. He wondered if Hank could still play his solo riff from memory.

Will chuckled to himself and felt a smile tug at his lips.

"Something funny?" Rick asked.

"Nah." Will shook his head. "Just thinking about Hank and me as kids. We did some stupid stuff."

Jake glanced at him then back at the road. "I thought Dad was going to blow a gasket the time the two of you rode your bikes through half the flower beds in the neighborhood."

"He did blow a gasket." He'd never forget how angry his father had been when one neighbor after another called to demand he do something about his unruly kid. "He took my bike away for the rest of the summer and made me replant every flower we'd run over."

"Hank was right beside you, as I recall," Rick said.

"He was. His parents weren't any happier than Dad was."

"That wasn't all Dad did." Jake twisted his hand on the steering wheel.

"No, it wasn't." Will had missed riding his bike the rest of the summer, but he'd missed his art supplies more. If there was one thing his dad knew how to do, it was punishing his kids. He knew their weaknesses and went right for them. Thankfully, he had his brothers. They'd stuck together—a united front against what had sometimes been cruel treatment. A lump formed in his throat as he recalled how he'd made it through those months. Rick and Jake had risked punishment and smuggled their own art supplies to him. They hadn't had much—colored pencils and crayons—but it had been better than nothing, and they'd known it. Here they were, saving his ass once again.

"Did I say thank you?" he asked, knowing it didn't matter if he had or not. His brothers didn't expect thanks, but he couldn't say it enough. No matter what, they had his back just as he had theirs.

"Yeah, you did." Rick who'd taken the rear seat so Will could ride shotgun nudged him in the shoulder. "So, don't mention it again."

He wasn't promising anything.

They pulled into the driveway of their childhood home. His neck muscles tightened. The place looked the same on the outside, but the inside had recently undergone a complete restoration—thanks to Rick's hard work. "Needs paint," he said past the lump in his throat as his crushed dreams pressed heavy on his shoulders.

"I was saving the job for you." Rick opened his door and piled out as soon as the car came to a stop.

Will took a deep breath before joining him. He'd had such big dreams when he left here all those years ago, and those dreams had taken him to places he hadn't known existed until he'd left small-town life behind. "White, as usual, with black shutters."

"Blue shutters, asshole." Jake joined them in front of the house.

"Black," Rick reiterated.

Will studied the familiar sight. "Does it matter? It's a fucking house."

"It matters if we're going to sell it." Jake had been advocating liquidation since they'd inherited the place. "It needs to stand out from the others."

A quick glance at the houses on either side supported Jake's vision. "He's right. Blue or green or something shocking like red will make the house stand out on the street." Will smiled at Rick's stunned expression.

"Standing out is not necessarily a good thing," his younger brother said as he returned to the car for Will's luggage.

Jake caught Will's gaze, and with a shrug, the two parted—Jake to unlock the front door and Will to help with his worldly goods.

Rick was putting on a good face, but something wasn't sitting right with him, and Will thought he knew what it was. Jake wanted to sell the house and Rick didn't. Will didn't give a shit what they did with it. Jake had never returned to live in the house after he'd left for college, opting to buy a place of his own on the other side of town when he'd returned to take over their father's law practice following the old man's death. Will had only spent a handful of nights in the house since he'd gone off to New York to pursue a career in the art world. Of the three of them, Rick was the only one who had any kind of attachment to the place. On the rare occasions Rick had come home to visit, he'd stayed with their dad, sleeping in the room the three brothers had shared growing up. When Rick had returned home for good, a silent and sullen man with no direction and even less ambition, his older brothers had seized on the sorry state of the house Rick insisted on living in as a form of therapy for him. They'd supplied him with paint, tools, and a modest budget to fix the place up. To their surprise, he'd thrown himself wholeheartedly into the project—or so it seemed from the pictures Jake had sent over the last few months.

"I can't wait to see what you've done inside." Will shoulder-nudged Rick out of the way and reached for his duffel.

"It's looking good if I do say so myself." Rick hefted Will's box of art supplies from the trunk then shut the lid. "You can have our old room. I've been sleeping in Dad's old room since I got it fixed up."

"Please tell me you got rid of the bunk beds in our room." He'd had a king-sized bed all to himself for years. Just thinking about folding himself into a small bunk bed for the foreseeable future made his back hurt. Or maybe it was the heavy bag he'd slung over his shoulder.

"Gone. The room wasn't big enough for anything but a full-size though. Sorry."

Will stifled a groan. None of this was Rick's fault so no need griping about his circumstances. He'd take what he could get and be happy about it. "I'm sure it'll be fine."

"*Fine* might be stretching the truth," Rick teased, "but it's better than the bunk beds we used to have." He held the front door open for Will. "It's a miracle I'm still alive. Those beds were cheap to begin with and we weren't gentle on them. I'm surprised you didn't crash down on me at some point and smoosh me."

Will smiled. "It wasn't for lack of trying. There were times I dreamed of ways to end your life."

"Like the time you put paprika on my toast instead of cinnamon?"

"It wouldn't have killed you," Jake said, taking the box from Rick's arms and placing it on the floor of the hall closet.

"You were in on it, too?" Rick placed his fists on his hips and glared at Jake.

"What can I say?" Jake straightened. "You were a brat. Always up in my and Will's business."

"Was not."

"Yes, you were." Will dropped his bag on the floor and slowly took in the new decor. Rick had refinished the hardwood floors, giving them a darker stain to contrast the light wall color. He kicked off his shoes and dug his toes into the soft pile of the new contemporary rug Rick had used to define the seating area. He ran a hand over the back of the mid-century sofa that fit the clean lines of the house better than the old Early American furniture ever had. A trio of his early paintings hung on the far wall above a couple of chairs that matched the sofa. He recalled sending the paintings to Rick for his birthday in lieu of a real present. It had been Will's first year at college in New York. He'd been full of himself and short on cash. He couldn't believe his brother had kept them, much less displayed them in his home, and this was very much

Rick's home now. No wonder he didn't want to sell the place. "Wow, little brother. This is awesome. Who would have thought?"

"I know, right?" Rick waved him on. "Come see what I did to the kitchen."

"You aren't going to believe this," Jake said, trailing behind his younger brothers.

Will stopped cold, blocking the door to the kitchen. If he hadn't seen the outside, he wouldn't have believed he was in the same house.

"I thought about knocking the wall out to create an open floor plan, but I didn't want to change the architecture of the house, so I settled for changing the layout. What do you think?"

"This is...incredible." Will took in the Shaker-style cabinets, new appliances, and countertops. "You did good, bro. Real good."

Jake shoved past him. "Want to see the best part of this room?" Before Will could answer, his older brother yanked on a cabinet handle. A large panel opened to reveal a refrigerator stocked with the essentials. "Who wants a beer?" he said, grabbing three bottles.

Will had dreaded returning to this house, dreaded the memories, but as he sat around the sleek new table in the eat-in kitchen, sipping ice-cold brews with his brothers, he was surprised to find they didn't come. Yeah, there were memories, but most of them were good ones. He wondered if his brother had weaved some sort of magic, throwing out the bad along with the old décor. If so, he was a genius. Will hadn't thought there was a chance in hell he'd feel comfortable in this house, but he was. And so was Rick. Only Jake looked like a prisoner eyeing the door, ready to escape any minute.

It was no wonder. Jake had taken the brunt of their father's abuse. No one had called it abuse back then. They'd called it *stern parenting. Making men out of boys.* Everyone knew better nowadays. Somehow, they'd all survived to varying degrees. Jake, if not ecstatically happy, seemed settled even though he was basically living their father's life—carrying on his law practice in the same offices in the same town with the same clients. Then there was Rick. He'd served his country with distinction and come home with wounds no one could see or touch. In rebuilding this house, he'd rebuilt himself. It was good to see him smile and joke again, particularly in this house that hadn't seen much of either since their mother had passed away. As far as Will knew, Rick hadn't dated since he returned home, and he hadn't mentioned anyone special in all the years he'd been serving the country.

"There's something I wanted to talk to you guys about," Rick said, drawing the brother's attention.

Will finished his beer, tossed the empty in the new built-in recycle bin then got them all fresh bottles. "This sounds serious. What's up?"

"As you can tell, I'm almost done here. Unless we add a second floor, there isn't anything left to do."

"Do you want to add a second floor?" Jake asked.

"Hell, no! Are you insane?" Rick glanced at his feet then lifted his eyes to his brothers. "Don't think I'm not grateful for all the two of you have done for me. I didn't know what to do with myself when I came home. This remodel gave me something to do with my hands while my head caught up." He stood and propped his hip against the counter, arms crossed over his chest. "But it's time for me to move on."

Will's heart jumped into his throat. His brother was leaving? What the hell? "To where?"

Rick cocked his head to one side. "Down the street. Henry Travis contracted me to remodel his kitchen."

"He did?" God, he could barely hear himself speak over the blood pounding in his ears. "When did this happen?"

Rick shrugged. "Couple of weeks ago. He's been stopping in a few days a week ever since I started working on the house. He'd talk while I worked. I think he's lonely. Hank got married. The old lady next door to him—"

"Miriam Wallingford," Jake supplied.

"Yeah, she's the one. She married Jonathan Youngblood and is living in England most of the year now. Anyway, Henry's going to travel some. See the world. He's renting the house out, and he asked if I'd be interested in remodeling the kitchen. It won't be anything as elaborate as this, I'll be staying within the existing footprint, but it's a complete remodel."

"Don't you have to have a contractor's license to do remodeling?" Leave it to Jake to ask the practical questions.

Rick's face turned red. "I have one. Been studying in the evenings. I took the exam a couple of weeks ago and passed."

Will couldn't hide his surprise or his happiness. He smiled and lifted his beer in a toast. "Way to go, bro! That's awesome."

"I didn't want to tell you guys—in case I lost my nerve or failed. I'll have to sub the electrical and plumbing work, but I'll do everything else myself. I gave him a really good price, seeing as he's my first customer. You know, see how this goes. If it works out, maybe I'll look for another job."

He was ecstatic about Rick's newfound ambition, but worrying about his little brother had become ingrained in his DNA. "Are you sure you're up to this? A few months ago—"

"I was a mess. I know." He ran his fingers through his overly long hair. "I don't know if I'll ever be the same person I was before, but I'm coping. Taking one day at a time. I know I can do the work. I don't know how I'll handle the stress of being in business for myself, but I managed to get through the contractor's exam without having a meltdown."

Will nodded. He could imagine the guts it had taken for Rick to step out of his comfort zone and take the test. His brother was slowly working his way back to a normal existence. He wished he had some of his brother's fortitude. "Okay, then."

"Wait a second." Jake had a propensity to beat every subject with a hammer until it was dead. "Who's Mr. Travis renting his place to? Are they going to be a problem?"

"She's the new PR person for BlackWing. I haven't met her yet. Gonna live in it during the remodel, too."

"You okay working around a tenant?"

Rick shuffled his feet. "Don't have a choice."

"You could say you changed your mind about doing the job."

"No. I need to do this. Need to see if I can. Besides, it's not like she'll be watching over my shoulder. She'll be at work when I'm at the house."

Will nodded his acceptance. His brother had made up his mind, and who was he to throw a monkey wrench into Rick's plans? Rick making plans was a monumental step in the right direction. "Well, I'm glad you have something to look forward to. When do you start?"

"Couple of weeks. Thought I'd let the new tenant settle in a bit before I start ripping things out."

"Have you drawn up a business plan? Filed for a DBA?" Jake went into full-lawyer mode, peppering Rick with questions. Will expected his younger brother to be upset by the detailed questioning, but he took it all in stride. His little brother was getting his shit together which made his own lack of planning seem worse in comparison.

CHAPTER FOUR

"MacKenzie, this is my wife, Melody Ravenswood Travis." Hank Travis smiled at the gorgeous brunette who'd just joined them in the recording studio. "Mel, this is our new PR guru, MacKenzie Carlysle."

Melody extended a slim hand. "So nice to finally meet you," she said as Kenzie took her hand. "Please, call me Mel. Sunny has nothing but good things to say about you."

"Thanks. Please, both of you, call me Kenzie, and Sunny filled my ear about the two of you and all the band members. I can't believe she didn't tell me she knew you until I cried on her shoulder about needing a job."

"Sunny was just honoring our wishes. Despite Hank's high-profile career and my not-so-secret background, we're pretty private people—as you can tell by the way we live. The middle of nowhere suits us, and we hope it will suit you, too."

Kenzie wasn't so sure about being suited to this kind of life, but if there was a paycheck involved, she was all for it...for now. Sunny had been right, Hank and Melody were lovely people who just happened to be famous, much like Sunny who was the daughter of one of Hollywood's favorite sons. "I grew up in D.C., moved to Manhattan for college then stayed there to work. I've never lived in a small town before. I'm looking forward to it."

"I speak for the entire band," Hank said. "We're glad to have you on board. Our agent has been filling in since Jason retired. With the new album dropping in a few months, we need someone who knows what they're doing."

"I've never worked in the music industry, but I'll give it all I've got. You won't be disappointed."

"Excellent. We couldn't ask for more. Jason left a ton of files for you." He indicated the file cabinets behind her new desk. "You'll find a lot of answers there, and Jase is only a phone call away. Feel free to ask us anything. Now, if you'll excuse me, I've got a song to write. Melody will bring you up to speed on the rest." With a kiss for his wife and a wave to Kenzie, Hank Travis left the women alone to talk.

"Wow." Kenzie let out a nervous breath as she turned to survey her new office space. It wasn't much, but it had all the necessities, including a window with a view of...crops. What kind, she didn't know or care. "I'm really here."

"Yes, you are." Melody waved Kenzie to her place behind the desk then took one of the visitors' chairs facing the desk. "How does it feel?"

Kenzie frowned.

"The chair?" Mel clarified. "It was Jason's. If it doesn't fit you, we'll get a new one. In fact, make a list of things you need and we'll get them for you. We want you to be comfortable."

"Thanks." The chair squeaked, and Jason's butt print didn't match her own. A new chair would top her list of needs. Other than proper seating, she couldn't think of a single thing she needed.

"Oh, and we ordered a new cell phone for you. It should be here tomorrow. It will have unlimited everything, so feel free to use it for your personal calls, too. The computer system here is state-of-the-art, but if there are any programs you need, put them on your new company credit card. We need to stop by the bank and pick your card up. Your new company car should be delivered to your house today."

"House?" Kenzie's head reeled with all the information coming in.

Mel's smile lit up her face. "I found a place for you to rent. Well, I didn't exactly find it. It sort of dropped in my lap. It's the perfect place. Not too big, not too small."

She had all Kenzie's attention. "I can't wait to see it. Where is it? When can I move in?"

"It's Hank's dad's house. It's in an older neighborhood, but all the houses are so cute and well-kept. You can move in today."

"Wait. What about Mr. Travis?"

"He's decided to do some traveling. He said he wants to see the world while he still can. He's starting out in England. He's going to stay at Ravenswood with Jonathan and Miriam for a little while."

Kenzie had heard all about Ravenswood, the ancient stone monstrosity Melody had inherited from her father. Since Earl Ravenswood's death, his best friend and former band-mate, Sir Jonathan Youngblood, had managed the singer's estate from his ancestral home. The place was high on Kenzie's list of places to visit if she ever got the chance.

"Is he coming back?" Kenzie wasn't sure she was going to stay here long, but she didn't want to bounce around like a rubber ball, either.

"Of course he is. His only child and his granddaughter are here. But don't worry." She waved her hand. "He'll either stay at Miriam's place, which is next door, or he'll stay with us."

"Sunny mentioned Mr. Travis' next-door neighbor married Jonathan Youngblood."

Mel nodded. "Miriam still has her house here. She and Uncle Jonathan split their time between Ravenswood and Willowbrook; otherwise, you could have rented her house."

"What about furniture?"

"Truthfully, it was all pretty old. I don't think he's bought so much as a new chair after his wife died. Hank convinced him to donate most of it and store the few pieces he couldn't part with."

"I doubt I'll have overnight guests, but I will need a bedroom set for myself, a kitchen table, and some living room furniture."

"No worries. Put it all on your company credit card. Pick whatever you like and consider it a signing bonus from the band. We're so glad to have you, Kenzie. You can't imagine what a burden you're lifting from Hank's shoulders."

"That's really generous." She didn't know what else to say. Her last employer had bought her a new blotter for her desk. She'd had to supply her own pens and staples. Cecil's penny-pinching ways should have been her first clue to his character.

"Oh," Melody said, "Henry—Hank's dad—said you could paint the walls. Even said he'd pay to have any work done you want to do. He'd already had plans drawn up to refurbish the kitchen and the bathroom before the travel bug bit him. If you'll supervise the remodel, he'll cut your rent in half until it's completed."

"What's the rent?"

Melody named a figure. "Half during the remodel."

"That's nothing, practically. Are you sure you got the amount right?"

"Positive. Henry doesn't need the money. He just wants someone to take care of the place and be there to keep an eye on the progress. With Miriam's house next door being unoccupied half the year, he's afraid to leave his empty, too."

"Makes sense, though I don't know about living next to an empty house. Does someone keep up with the maintenance?"

"Yep. Uncle Jonathan had a security system installed and hired a local company to take care of the landscaping year-round. Oh, and we have a key in case we need to use the house for overflow."

"Overflow?"

"When BlackWing is recording, there's not enough room at our place for the band, their families, and all the extra musicians and technical people who come in. We used to send them to Henry's house, but with you living there...well, we didn't think you'd appreciate the company."

"Depends on who you send over," Kenzie said, with a grin. Her spirits were lifting higher with each new revelation from her new employer's mouth. "If they're hot and single, I wouldn't mind."

Melody shook her head. "You're going to fit right in with Black-Wing, I can tell."

"Thanks. I'm excited about being part of the team." She was. Really. It was the move and getting used to small-town life…and leaving behind everything leading up to her departure from New York. Once she got past it all, she was sure she'd find her footing in Willowbrook. Or maybe Dallas. She still held out hope she could convince Hank to let her work from home.

"Oh, good. Your car's here." Melody pulled to the curb in front of a small white bungalow on Pecan Street.

Kenzie couldn't believe her eyes. This was going to be her home? She'd fallen a little in love with this neighborhood when her limo driver had given her a tour of the town, but never in her wildest dreams had she thought she would live here. A city girl all her life, the tree-lined streets with their quietly unassuming houses were reminiscent of another time, a simpler life she'd never known would appeal to her—until now.

Kenzie stepped from Mel's Jeep to the shaded walkway and stared at her new home.

The house itself appeared much like all the others on the street, white with black shutters on the windows. Pots and hanging baskets filled with flowering plants adorned the wide front porch. An old-fashioned screened door was flanked by rocking chairs on one side and a swing on the other. Flower beds skirted the front of the house, providing vibrant color against the backdrop of the house and the perfect green lawn. Like a movie set—it was almost too good to be true.

She focused on the neatly edged grass. She couldn't wait to take her shoes off and walk barefoot across it. "I've never had a lawn."

"Don't worry. We hired the same landscape company Miriam and Jonathan use to do yours, too. I think they come on Friday, but don't quote me on that. I have their card somewhere. I'll hunt it up for you. If you need to change the date or time they're here or need something specific done, give them a call.

"Thanks." She'd be grateful for the help, but, seeing the neat flower beds, she thought she might like to give gardening a try.

As if she'd read Kenzie's mind, Mel added, "There's a little garden in the back where Hank's mother used to grow a few vegetables. Henry has kept the weeds and grass out, but it's been years since anyone planted anything there. Feel free to try your hand at some flowers or veggies."

She'd fallen down a rabbit hole. It was the only explanation for all of this. The job. The house. The car. A garden for crying out loud! What was happening to her? First, she'd hooked up with a stranger in the airport—something she should regret but couldn't bring herself to—now she was thinking about gardening. Next, she'd be carrying on a conversation with a cat and attending a tea party.

"Come on." Mel started up the walk to the porch. "Let's see what Henry left in the way of kitchen stuff." She paused on the porch and dug around in her giant purse, eventually coming up with a leather-bound notepad and a pen. "We'll make a list then we'll go shopping."

CHAPTER FIVE

"I've got a bed, a sofa, and a TV. What else do I need?" Kenzie never thought she'd complain about shopping, but she couldn't stop the words from spewing past her lips. She and Mel had done nothing but shop for the last three days. Hank insisted there was plenty of time, but Kenzie was dying to dive headfirst into her new job. Apparently, it wasn't happening today. Currently, they were on their way to the local diner to have lunch with Mel and Hank's friend, Cathy, who owned The Donut Hole on Main Street. Mel had been in there every morning so far and was quickly becoming addicted to their chocolate croissants and dark-roast coffee.

"Curtains, for one thing, and we need to choose paint colors for all the rooms." Mel set a brisk pace any New Yorker would be proud of. "You said yourself the wall colors were dingy."

She had commented on the wall paint, but she was beginning to regret opening her mouth. If she'd known Mel was going to drag her all over North Texas, looking for furnishings, and now, paint, she would have kept her mouth shut and lived with the dull interior finishes. A few cheap prints on the walls would brighten the place up enough for now. She'd already ordered a few from an online art catalog and charged them to her personal charge card. She'd admired the artist's work for years, but when she'd just started out on her own in New York, she hadn't been able to afford even a small print. Once she'd had the funds to purchase whatever she wanted, she'd had no place to hang one. She'd lived in her former boyfriend's loft, and, as an art dealer, every available space had been covered with originals from the artists he admired. There'd been no room for her favorites. She should have realized then what a bastard Cecil was, but she'd been in love—stupid blind love. Until his deceit had restored her vision to 20/20.

She could see clearly now. No more relationships. Just sex. Visions of Hot Airport Guy popped into her brain, making her heart trip all over itself. Why, oh why, did he keep coming to mind? It had been quick, hot, and extremely satisfying sex. Nothing more. End of interlude. End of discussion. So why couldn't she move past it? It wasn't like she was ever going to see him again. He'd gone his way. She'd gone hers. Their paths would never cross again.

"Cathy's good with colors. I'd never dream of choosing a paint color without her input." Mel tugged the door to the diner open. Kenzie followed her inside.

Heavenly aromas greeted the women. Mel may have been immune, but Kenzie inhaled deeply, sure she'd gain several pounds just from the smell of deep-fried everything and home-baked desserts. Her stomach growled, reminding her how long it had been since she'd last eaten.

"There she is!" Mel waved at the woman leaning out of one of the window-front booths. "Come on. You'll love Cathy. She's the greatest."

Like everything else in Willowbrook, the place could double as a set for a 1950s era movie. They crossed the black-and-white checkered floor, weaving through a maze of four-top tables with mismatched chairs and tabletop jukeboxes. So far, everyone Kenzie had met in town had been warm and friendly despite her being a Yankee. She didn't doubt Cathy would live up to Mel's hype.

Mel made the introductions then the two of them slid into the opposite side of the booth from the donut shop owner. Kenzie had expected someone as big as a barn, but Cathy was slim and absolutely gorgeous with a smile to put anyone instantly at ease.

"It's nice to officially meet you," Kenzie said. "I've been in your shop nearly every day this week."

"Really?" Cathy's smile grew brighter. "I hope you're addicted." She directed her next comment to Mel. "I hear I've lost one of my best customers."

Melody adjusted her purse on the seat between them. "If you're talking about Henry, it's temporary. He wants to see a little bit of the world while he still can." She passed out menus from the holder next to the window. "Hank's worried about his dad traveling alone, but nothing we said was enough to convince him to stay."

Cathy opened her menu. "I understand where Henry's coming from. If I were in his shoes, I'd do the same thing. I'm sure glad he found me a replacement for the lost business though." She winked at Kenzie.

"I don't know how many donuts Mr. Travis bought, but I'll do my best to keep up." It wouldn't be difficult. Everything she'd tried at The Donut Hole had been to die for. She needed to find a gym soon, or she'd be a dumpling in no time.

"Well, well, well. Would you look at that?"

Kenzie glanced up from her menu to see what Cathy was talking about. A trio of sexy men walked single file past the counter seating complete with a view of the kitchen pass-through to the circular booth in the back corner of the café. Tall, dark, and brooding, they each had a distinctive style, yet they moved as one cohesive unit. Any woman who didn't sit up and take notice of such a fine display of manhood needed hormone supplements. Her lady parts were doing just fine—thank you very much. No assistance needed. Especially where the one in the middle was concerned. *Lord have mercy. It's* him.

Even from this distance, she could see flecks of white paint in his hair. His tattered, paint-splattered T-shirt and equally ratty jeans hugged and defined every muscle of his lean body. Not exactly the urban chic guy she'd hooked up with in the Philly airport—but it *was* him. No doubt about it. Her core melted as the visceral memories of what she'd done with the man incinerated the mental box she'd placed them in, scorching her from the inside out. Heart hammering, Kenzie ducked back behind her menu, hoping against hope he hadn't seen her. *What is he doing here anyway?* The city girl in her immediately wondered if he'd followed her, but she immediately swatted the thought away like she would a pesky fly. A covert peek told her the guys he was with today were the same ones he'd met at the airport. What were the odds they were just passing through Willowbrook today and stopped for a bite to eat? Her gut told her it wasn't the case, and Mel confirmed it.

"It's the brothers Grim."

Kenzie's gaze snapped to her friend. "Grimm? As in the fairy tales?"

"Their real last name is Ingram," Melody clarified.

"Grim as in ghastly, gloomy, and glum," Cathy offered.

"They live here?" *Please don't say yes.*

"'Fraid so." Cathy closed her menu, set it back in the holder then drummed her fingers on the table's red Formica surface. "They haven't always been grim."

"You know them?" Of course Cathy knew them. If there was one thing she'd figured out in the week or so she'd been a resident of Willowbrook, it was that everyone knew everyone else. She didn't know how long she was going to live here, but if it was longer than another seven days, her path was going to cross with his. Best to know what she was up against, so she could avoid running into him as much as possible.

"Do they have names?" She couldn't go on calling him Hot Guy from the airport.

Mel set her menu aside. "Jake, Will, and Rick. Jake's the oldest and Rick's the youngest."

Instinct, or something more, made Kenzie glance toward the brothers. Her breath caught in her throat. The brothers were looking their way. The one on the far left of the semicircle booth clenched his jaw before returning his gaze to the menu he held open in front of him. Opposite him, another Grim brother shook his head slightly then flipped his menu open. Kenzie's gaze fell on the one sandwiched between the other two. His dark gaze met hers, and, instantly, she knew he knew. Just like in the airport, her brain registered danger, but her body responded like she'd stuck her finger in a light socket while standing in a puddle of murky water.

Oh, he was a dangerous one all right. It was there, in those dark orbs that both threatened and promised with a single look. His broad shoulders filled the space allotted him by his brothers. Was his hair longer, or was it her imagination? She clenched her hands into fists as her fingers itched to see if the dark strands were as soft as they appeared. He'd had a bit of scruff on his jaw when she last saw him, but she was beginning to think he didn't own a razor. The style was sexy as hell on him. Damn. She had it bad if she didn't care he'd gone from GQ model to blue-collar heathen. She still wanted him more than she should. More than was prudent. More than was sane.

Mel waved a hand in front of Kenzie's face, forcing her to break contact. "Earth to MacKenzie. Earth to MacKenzie. Come in, Kenzie."

Another quick glance told her the game was over. Hot Guy hid behind his menu. With a silent sigh, she focused on her lunch companions. "What? Can't a girl look?"

Cathy leaned across the table. "You won't get anywhere with those guys. No one ever does."

Kenzie raised one eyebrow. "Do you speak from experience?" *Please don't tell me she's been with him.* Kenzie didn't want him. She really didn't, no matter what her lower body was telling her. But the idea of any woman having him, especially one she'd just met, unleashed something primal and possessive within. What was it about him that made her go cavewoman?

"No," Cathy insisted. "But I know others who have tried to put a smile on one of those faces. Every single one ended in disaster."

Recalling the intensity of her recent Grim stare-down, she thought smiles might be overrated. There was something to be said for determination and commitment to a goal. Hot Guy had both in spades. He'd proved as much in Philly. "How so? Details, please."

Uttering a long sigh, Cathy sat back. "The stories aren't mine to tell, but I can say any attempts to reform Jake and Rick have been unsuccessful. It's as if they don't want to be happy. And from what I hear, since Will returned last week, he fits right into the family mold."

A waitress wearing a pink-polyester dress, complete with a white collar and the pointed tips of a fake handkerchief poking from a breast pocket, stopped at their table, pencil and green order pad at the ready. A white oval name tag said, "Penny."

"Hey, Mel," Penny said.

"Hi, Pen." Mel gestured across the table. "This is the new PR person we hired for BlackWing. MacKenzie Carlysle, Penny Michaels."

Penny's gaze swung to Kenzie. "Nice to meet you." Tossing her head to indicate the brothers Grim, she waggled her eyebrows. "Saw you checking them out. They're our version of Mt. Rushmore. Bigger than life but cold and hard as stone."

She could see the hard-as-stone bit—and personally testify to the accuracy of the statement in regard to one of them—but cold? No way. She recalled the feel of Will gripping her hips as he drove into her over and over again. After he'd left, she'd checked to see if he'd branded her and been somewhat sad to see he hadn't. Not in any physical way, but he'd imprinted on her brain. As much as she'd tried, she hadn't been able to get him out of her mind. She fanned herself with the menu as she smiled up at the waitress. "And not easily accessible?"

"Many have tried. None have succeeded."

"Told you so," Cathy smirked.

Kenzie laughed. There wasn't a thing she could do about her present situation, so it was time to change the subject. "I'll have a cheeseburger, fries, and a diet soda." She placed her menu back in the rack.

"Excellent choice." Penny asked the requisite questions to complete the order then turned to Kenzie's lunch companions. "The usual?"

"Chicken Caesar salad and sweet tea," Mel confirmed.

Cathy took one last look at the menu then, with a sigh, slapped it shut. "Who am I kidding? I'll have the usual—the cheddar bacon burger and sweet potato fries."

"Diet soda?"

"Yep," Cathy said.

Penny scribbled on her pad then tucked her pencil behind her ear before nodding discreetly at the table across the way. "They weren't always grim," she said. "Cathy can tell you. She dated Rick in high school." Penny cruised over to take the brothers' orders as if she hadn't just tossed a flash/bang grenade in the middle of their table.

Once Kenzie picked her jaw up off the floor, she narrowed her eyes at the woman who'd, moments ago, denied any intimate knowledge of the brothers.

"You dated Rick in high school?" She leaned in closer.

"Yes, I dated Rick Ingram," she said, sounding anything but happy about it. "I went out with Hank Travis a couple of times, too." She flashed an apologetic smile in Melody's direction.

Mel patted Cathy's hand. "I thank you for not sleeping with my future husband when you had the chance."

"You're welcome, though if the offer had included better accommodations and/or a ring, I might have made a different decision."

Mel leaned over and half-whispered to Kenzie. "He offered her a romp in the bed of his pickup." She rolled her eyes. "Can't imagine why she passed on the offer. Can you?"

"Nope." Squelching an urge to laugh out loud, Kenzie shook her head. "Sounds like a pretty good offer, knowing the source." Melody's husband, Hank Travis, besides being Kenzie's new boss, was sexy as hell. Not to mention he was the drummer for BlackWing, one of the hottest rock bands in the country.

"You didn't know Hank then," Cathy said. "Who knew he'd turn out to be a rock star?"

Melody relaxed in the booth. "He asks the same question all the time. But it's what he was meant to do."

Kenzie had to agree with Mel's assessment. Hank Travis was crazy talented. "Enough about Hank." She cocked her head toward the table full of single hunks. "Which one of those is Rick?"

"The one on the right," Cathy said without turning to check.

Kenzie could just see him past Penny's polyester-clad hips. Broad shoulders like his brothers. Hair way too long for convention. His clean-shaven jaw resembled the stone monument Penny had referenced. Thanks to the way the waitress held her arms while she wrote on her order pad, Kenzie couldn't see Rick's eyes, but she could see his hand, clenched in a tight fist, sitting atop a tree-trunk thigh. *Damn.*

"You let *him* get away?"

"I didn't *let* him do anything," she said. "It was his dream to go to the Naval Academy. When he got in, he left and never looked back."

Oh, there was a story there, one she fully intended to hear—in great detail—later on. For now, she'd settle for the broader picture.

"So tell me," Kenzie said. "What happened to make the brothers so glum?"

"Don't know, exactly." Cathy slipped her flatware from its napkin cocoon. Smoothing the white embossed paper over her lap, she continued. "Jake is the oldest. He was a few years ahead of me. William graduated a year ahead of me in Hank's class. Rick's my age, and the youngest of the bunch. There's little more than a year between each of them. Stairsteps, as my mom would say.

"Their mom passed away, cancer, I think, when Rick and I were in middle school. No. Wait. It was our last year of elementary school. I remember because he missed a lot of classes and had to go to summer school to make up the time. My mom was the teacher that summer.

She'd come home with a story to tell almost every day about something Rick had done or said."

"He was acting out?"

"I don't know. Maybe." Cathy moved the cheap knife and fork from the left of her placemat to the right.

Kenzie and Melody shared a look, reaching an unspoken agreement to pry the rest of the story out of the woman with a bottle of wine and chocolate later on. Right then, Kenzie wanted all the intelligence she could get on the other two brothers, particularly the one in the middle.

Penny arrived with their food, temporarily distracting them from the subject of the Ingram brothers. Kenzie groaned as she chewed and swallowed her first bite. "Oh. My. God. This has got to be the best cheeseburger I've ever eaten," she said, wiping greasy drippings off her chin.

Melody laughed. "Keep it down, girlfriend. People are going to wonder what's going on over here!"

Kenzie swirled a thick French fry in a puddle of ketchup and brought it to her lips, painting them with the sauce before opening her mouth to take the fried spud in. "Mmm. This is good, too. Soooo good," she crooned.

"Stop it." Mel blushed at the same time she kicked Kenzie under the table. "People are staring."

"What people?" Glancing around, her gaze met and locked with eyes belonging to Hot Guy.

Oh god. Staring wasn't even close to the right word for the way he was watching her. Involuntarily licking her lips, she swallowed hard past her heart which had lodged itself in her throat and forced her attention back to the plate of food she no longer wanted. Yes, she was hungry, but not for food. Everything she wanted was on the other side of the restaurant, and if looks could convey a message, he wanted her, too.

Trying her best to appear unaffected by his gaze, Kenzie popped another fry into her mouth and washed it past the now-massive obstruction in her throat with a swig of her soda. She turned to Cathy. "You were telling me about the brothers Grim. Did the other two go into the military as well?"

Cathy took a quick sip from her glass. "Nope. Jake, he's the one on the left, is a lawyer. Took over their dad's practice here in town a couple of years ago after their dad passed away. William—the one in the middle—went to college in New York to study art. He'd always been the quiet one of the bunch, but at least he used to smile. I thought he was doing well, selling paintings left and right." She shrugged. "Don't know what happened, but word on the street is he's back to stay."

Kenzie froze, the straw sticking out of her soda just a few centimeters from her lips. A hodge-podge of memories flashed through her brain. Paintings. Ingram. The sexy guy on the cover of the New Yorker magazine. Her vision clouded, and she forced herself to breathe as the impossible became highly likely. Her hand shook as she placed her beverage back on the table. "Wait just one minute."

She fought for enough breath to voice what she was almost certain was the truth. It defied explanation but was undoubtedly another chapter in the shit-show her life had become. Leaning in, she whispered, "You're telling me, the man sitting over there—William Ingram—is W.H. Ingram? The artist?"

Before either woman could answer, the images flitting around in her brain coalesced into one.

Oh. My. God.

I had airport sex with W. H. Ingram.

Did he know who I was when he accepted my offer? Suddenly, it all made sense. He was way out of her league when it came to sexual partners. She'd known it then and hoped for the best—and been somewhat stunned when he'd agreed to a hookup. *And why wouldn't he? I fucked him over, and he'd returned the favor. Those glorious moments in the Philly airport were a revenge fuck.*

Thanks to the giant lump still in her throat, Kenzie was able to stifle the groan of misery bubbling up from her gut.

Could my life get any more fucked-up?

"I seem to recall he signs his paintings as W. H.," Mel said. "I can ask him if you want?"

Apparently, it could. "No!" Kenzie recoiled at the sound of her voice raised beyond the acceptable level.

"Or, better yet, I'll look at the one in Hank's office."

Kenzie forced wind past her vocal chords. "Hank has a W.H. Ingram painting in his office?"

Mel nodded, her expression one of concern. "Yes," she replied cautiously. "I bought it from Sunny's gallery in New York a few years ago. That's how we met. I saw a painting in the window and bought it for Hank."

"Did you buy it because Will Ingram painted it?"

"I didn't know anything about the artist when I purchased it. I was walking down the sidewalk and saw it in the window of her gallery. It reminded me of Willowbrook, so I bought it for Hank, and a few others for myself. It wasn't until much later we realized it *was* Willowbrook and Will had painted it. Hank was impressed. He's been trying to buy another of Will's paintings but hasn't had any luck."

No. He wouldn't have any luck finding one unless the man had a secret stash of paintings no one knew about. *Like the ones that have gone missing?* She mentally shook her head. He hadn't taken his own paintings. She was 99 percent certain. He'd been a victim of two ruthless people, just as she had been, for reasons she still didn't understand and might never know. She recalled the paint splatters she'd seen on his clothes when he walked in. Had he resumed painting? The art world would be a better place if he had, but she'd heard he'd vowed he'd never lift a brush again. That kind of hurt was something she could relate to.

As much as she loved the art world, she didn't want to go back there. She had this opportunity to work in the music industry, and she was going to give it everything she had.

The part she'd played in the demise of Will's career was a small one, but it weighed heavy on her shoulders. She owed him an apology, but, after the revenge fuck, she doubted he'd be interested in anything she had to say.

She could at least explain why Hank couldn't find another W.H. Ingram to purchase. "He quit painting."

"I didn't know. Hank will be disappointed. Will is a talented artist."

"I agree." Cathy ate another of her fries. "I've seen the painting you're talking about. It's absolutely gorgeous. It should be in a museum."

"It probably should be." Sorrow laced Kenzie's words. "He's really good. Hang on to the painting, Mel. It's probably worth a lot more than what you paid for it, and when your daughter is grown, it will be worth a fortune."

"I don't care what its monetary value is. It's special to Hank and to me. We'll never part with it."

Kenzie pushed her plate away. "As delicious as this is, I can't eat another bite."

Cathy gaped at her. "You hardly touched it."

"I know. My eyes were bigger than my stomach, I guess." She took a couple of bills out of her wallet and placed them on the table. "I need to get a few things from the drugstore. Take your time." She scooted out of the booth and stood, grateful her legs held. "Meet me in front of the hardware store when you're through?"

Both women seemed perplexed at the abrupt change in her demeanor, but readily agreed to meet at the prescribed location midway between the diner and the drugstore. Kenzie squared her shoulders and bolted for the door as fast as she could without making a scene. With every step, she felt William H. Ingram's gaze burning a hole through her.

She'd deserved the revenge fuck. She deserved his hatred. She just wished there was some way to make up to him for what she'd done.

CHAPTER SIX

Will sensed *something* from the moment he'd stepped into the diner with his brothers. Once he'd located the source of the feeling, he couldn't take his eyes off the woman. *What the hell is she doing here? Is she following me? Is she a reporter?* The possibility punched him in the chest and stole his breath. But what would she be doing with those two?

He knew the ladies sitting across the booth from her. Cathy owned The Donut Hole a few doors down from here, and had been in Rick's graduating class, a year behind him. He'd known her most of his life. The other woman had moved to Willowbrook a couple of years ago. She'd been Melody Harper then, just a reporter for the local newspaper. The whole town had been stunned to find out she was the only child of Rock and Roll legend Earl Ravenswood. Her father's music as lead guitarist for RavensBlood had been the soundtrack for his youth and inspiration for Hank Travis, the man Melody had married. *Melody used to be a reporter. Is that how she knew the woman from the airport?*

Shit.

He hadn't told anyone except the police where he was going when he left New York. Had they leaked the information to one of the investigative reporters who'd sniffed around the case at the beginning—or worse—to one of the tabloids?

His brain cycled back to the airport bar and the way she'd approached him. Not the other way around. God, she must have thought he was an easy mark, and he had been. Fortunately for him, all he'd wanted was a quick fuck, a way to release some tension, and, yes, make sure the important parts were still in working order. For the last several months, desire had been in short supply. He hadn't hung around for pillow talk—something she'd probably counted on.

Bitch.

He had no desire to tell his story to anyone, though eventually he would tell Jake. There were things only a lawyer should ask interested parties, and Will had plenty of questions. Too bad he didn't know who had the answers. Maybe Jake could find out. The NYPD had done all they were going to do. Unless someone walked into a precinct with a stack of paintings and confessed to stealing them, they weren't going to spend another minute hunting for his property or the people responsible.

Jake's voice dragged Will out of the well of depression he'd fallen into. "Hey, Rick. Who's the looker sitting with your old girlfriend?"

"Dunno. Don't care," his younger brother replied. Opening his menu, Rick studied it like it held the secret code to happiness. Lord knew Rick needed the code. Hell, they all did. Life had served Rick a shitty hand. It had dumped a lifetime of bad luck on Will's head, and he didn't know what had crawled up his oldest brother's butt.

"Maybe you should care," Jake said. "She's checking us out."

Only she wasn't looking at Jake or Rick. Her focus was entirely on him. From across the crowded diner, he could tell her eyes were blue, the kind a man could get lost in, drown in. He should know. He'd almost drowned in them at an airport bar in Philly. His reaction to her gaze had been one of the motivating factors in the way he'd taken her later on. Eyes didn't lie. They didn't say I love you when they meant otherwise. He hadn't wanted to read her emotions, and he damn sure hadn't wanted her to read his. Though he was now questioning her motivations, all he'd wanted was emotionless sex, and the best way to ensure it remained strictly physical was to fuck her from behind. No eye contact. No words whispered in an ear. No kissing. Served her right for trying to weasel a story out of him. But he wasn't stupid. Not anymore, anyway. He'd learned his lesson about trusting women. It would take more than a good fuck to make him talk.

Will redirected his attention to the only people in his life who mattered—his brothers. Rick didn't need any shit from either of them. He was getting his life together in his own way. Pushing him toward a relationship he didn't want wasn't any way to help. "Mind your own business, big brother."

Not taking his gaze off his menu, Jake countered, "Both of you *are* my business."

"Like hell we are."

Jake's head jerked up, his gaze locking with Will's. Will continued, "When are you going to get it through your thick skull? We're grown men, Jake. Rick and I are no longer your responsibility. We never were."

Jake glared across the table, and his lips formed a thin white line across his flushed face. "If you're so grown up, why don't you act like it?"

What the hell was I thinking coming back here? This was the same argument they had nearly every time the brothers got together, and one seemingly with no resolution. Jake thought his position in the family gave him the right to boss his younger siblings around. Will and Rick thought otherwise.

"Hey," Rick said. "Can't we have lunch without you two arguing?"

Will forced his grip to loosen on the menu. One of these days, he was going to force Jake to loosen his grip on him and Rick, even if he had to beat him to a pulp to get his message across. This was not the time or the place to hang their dirty laundry out though. "Fine by me."

Jake held his gaze for a long moment then, with a sigh, focused on the lunch offerings. "Fine."

Will glanced at Rick. His little brother had been through hell and brought some of the demons home with him. He was doing a lot better than when he first got home, but he hated conflict. Even the harmless kind between siblings put shadows in his eyes. "Sorry," Will said.

"No problem." Rick pretended to read his menu.

Will kicked Jake under the table. His older brother jerked and turned on him. Before Jake could say a thing, Will cocked his head toward Rick and raised one brow. Thankfully, his oldest brother got the message.

"Sorry, Rick."

"No problem. Anybody else want a milkshake?"

"I'll have one," Will said.

"Me, too." Jake set his menu aside. "The bacon cheeseburger sounds good with sweet potato fries."

While Will kept cautious watch on the table across the way, the brothers discussed the merits of their lunch choices like normal folks. The way Penny stood while she took the ladies' orders blocked his view of the newcomer, but he could hear the lilt of her voice, as she conversed with the waitress. Definitely the woman from the airport. He could practically feel her soft skin beneath his hands and, if he closed his eyes, recall her scent on his fingers.

Fuck! He shouldn't be thinking of her, but there was no hope for it. He couldn't get her out of his mind.

His jeans grew uncomfortably tight, and he considered starting another argument with Jake to ease the unwanted pressure. One glance at Rick convinced him to come up with another way to deal with his problem. It was so rare to see his younger brother's face devoid of tension, he couldn't bring himself to wreck the moment.

How did we get to this point? Three angry men unable to have a meal together without cutting each other to shreds?

They'd been normal kids, once upon a time. They each had their reasons for the way they were now, reasons they hoarded like favorite toys, unwilling to share. Rick was short on specifics, but it didn't take a genius to see his years in the Navy had changed him. Jake apparently had taken himself on as a client and refused to divulge anything about his life to anyone. Will didn't need a shrink to tell him what had gone wrong in his life. He'd trusted a woman and gotten burned. Seared to the soul was more like it. It would be a cold day in hell before he'd make the same mistake again.

They'd barely gotten their plates when he saw her slide out of the booth and head for the door. Will looked at his cheeseburger then to the woman weaving her way through the scattering of tables, and made a snap decision.

Tossing his napkin on the table, he shoved Rick in the shoulder. "Move it, asshole. I need to get out."

"Hey, who you calling asshole?" Despite his irritation, Rick stood, allowing Will to slide out of the middle seat. "You sick or something?"

"Nah. I'll be back. Give me a minute."

He didn't want to explain to his brothers where he was going, or why, but he'd have to tell them something. Neither one was stupid. They'd see her walking out with him trailing behind, and there was nothing in the world to keep them from reaching conclusions. None of which would be correct, thus the reason he'd have to tell them something when he returned. For now, all he could think about was catching up to her and letting her know he wasn't the story she was looking for. The sooner she left for New York, the better.

He hit the glass door at a sprint, shoving it open with his shoulder as he craned his head both ways, searching for her. She wasn't difficult to find. She leaned against the wall of the hardware store next door, her face turned in his direction.

Damn. He'd fallen right into her trap. Followed her out like a puppy on a leash. And he'd thought he knew better.

Will closed the distance between them, his anger growing with each step. He'd left everything behind in New York, except, apparently, this one reporter. The sooner she left, the sooner he could get on with his new life—whatever his life was going to be.

He stopped, his toes inches from hers. Up close, his artist's eye took in the perfect structure of her features. His fingers itched to touch, to add a tactile memory to the visual one imprinted on his brain. To prevent the involuntarily motion, he stuffed his hands in his front pockets.

Any artist worth his salt would give anything to paint her. Anyone but him. He wasn't an artist any longer. Now he painted houses. He'd started with his childhood home and, thanks to Rick, now had another one down the street waiting for his brush. Nothing artistic about swabbing white paint on tired wood. It was all muscle and sweat. No brain power needed. It was exactly the kind of job he wanted from now on.

But, god, she made him want things he had no business wanting. Like in the airport. He'd wanted to fuck her. Hard. Had wanted to prove something to himself, and maybe to her for having the audacity to proposition him, a perfect stranger, in an airport bar.

Ah, but he hadn't been a stranger after all, had he? She'd known who he was all along. Had planned the whole thing in an attempt to get his side of the story. It would be a cold day in Hades before he told her anything.

He inhaled deeply. Her intoxicating scent filled his nostrils and damn near disintegrated his resolve to send her packing. Sunshine and flowers. It somehow suited her, and when he painted her, both would be represented. A vision of her naked, a shaft of morning light revealing her perfect features, soft and replete from a man's attentions, burst across his consciousness. His dick responded, hardening against his fly, wanting to be the man to put a satisfied look on her face. He wouldn't be, and the realization felt like a rusty knife had been thrust between his ribs.

Will stepped away, hoping some fresh air would clear his big brain of its stupid ideas. Before he lost control and followed through on one of his crazy thoughts, he forced the words he'd come to say past his lips. "I don't know who the hell you think you are, but I've got some advice for you. Go back to New York where you belong. There's nothing for you here."

"But—"

"No buts. I said all I was going to say in New York. I'm done talking. W.H. Ingram no longer exists. End of story. Tell that to your readers."

"But...I'm not a reporter. I swear."

Already halfway to the diner's door, her words stopped him cold. He turned. "Then who the hell are you?"

"No one you want to know, but I swear, I didn't follow you. I didn't even know who you were until Melody told me a few minutes ago."

"How do you know Melody Travis?" He stepped closer but stayed out of range of her scent. Whatever was going on here, he needed all his brain cells engaged.

"I don't, really. She's a new friend. She's helping me shop for furniture. I work for her husband, Hank. Well, technically, I work for Black-Wing. I'm MacKenzie, their new public relations person."

"You're telling me you didn't recognize me in the Philly airport?"

Her long hair swirled around her shoulders as she shook her head. "No. I swear. Our meeting was...spontaneous."

Well, shit. Will ran the fingers of one hand through his hair, murmuring a curse when they snagged on a clump of dried paint. *What a clusterfuck.* "Why did you hightail it out of the diner?"

"Uh." She bit her bottom lip and looked up at him through long lashes. "I don't know. Mel had just dropped the bomb about who you were, and, all of a sudden, it hit me—what I'd done in the airport. I couldn't just sit there and eat my burger like nothing had happened, and I couldn't *tell* them what happened, so I made up an excuse and left."

If she was lying, she deserved an Academy Award for her performance. But, then again, he'd fallen for another woman's lies and was still paying the price for his mistake. Time would tell if she was who she said she was. He backed toward the diner's door. "Tell Hank I said hello."

"Will do."

WILL

The moment he stepped inside the diner, he knew he'd made a tactical error. His brothers glanced up from their meals with expressions he should have predicted. Concern graced Rick's face. He always expected trouble, and, in this case, he was right. MacKenzie—he realized she hadn't given him her last name—was going to be trouble with a capital T. He could feel it in his bones. On the other side of their table, Jake's face radiated disapproval, reminding him so much of his father when Will had failed to live up to his expectations, he had the urge to turn around and leave. Fuck lunch. He could find something to snack on at the house.

"You want me to box your meal up for you?"

Will snapped his attention to Penny who had snuck up on him. Jake and Rick were almost finished eating. His would be cold, but what the hell? "No, but thanks. I'll finish it here." With a little luck, his brothers would go back to work and leave him in peace.

"No need to wait on me," he said as Rick stood to let him slide to his spot in the middle of the horseshoe-shaped booth. "I'll finish up and be along in a few."

"Fuck you." Rick settled into his seat. "What was that all about? You know her?"

The lyrics of an old country song came to mind. *If it weren't for bad luck, I'd have no luck at all.*

I should have it tattooed on my ass.

"No. She looked familiar though." It wasn't exactly a lie. He didn't know her. Hell, he still didn't know her last name. He knew plenty of other things about her, but he wasn't going to share those with anyone, especially his brothers.

Will popped a cold fry into his mouth and when he tried to find the ketchup container, his gaze locked with Jake's. *Shit.* The old Rick Ingram never would have let him off so easily, but this new version of his brother wasn't into confrontation. But Jake, the fucking lawyer, wasn't buying the mistaken identity excuse.

"Let it go, big brother." He glanced at his little brother. Rick was checking sports scores on his phone. Will caught Jake's gaze and mouthed, *later*. He wasn't happy about the delay, but Jake dipped his chin, acknowledging receipt of the message.

Every bite Will took felt like wet concrete sliding down his throat, but he didn't dare leave a scrap on his plate. Loss of appetite wouldn't go unnoticed by either brother. Rick didn't need the worry, and Jake didn't need any more ammunition. He'd heard a little about what had happened to Will. Both brothers had, but neither had the whole story. The police in New York had strongly advised him to have someone do some digging on his behalf. No one was dead—as far as they knew—so they weren't going to expend much manpower on the investigation. After a few weeks, all trails had gone cold and the file had been buried beneath a slew of new ones. Will simply hadn't had the funds to hire an investigator. He still didn't, but he had Jake. A call from a lawyer could loosen tongues and jog memories. It was the only shot he had at recovering any part of his career. Hell, he'd settle for getting some of his cash back. Fuck the paintings.

CHAPTER SEVEN

Kenzie's knees shook like limbs in a nor'easter as she watched William H. Ingram walk back inside the diner.

William. H. Ingram. Holy shit.

She still couldn't wrap her head around the fact he lived in Willowbrook or how she'd propositioned him in an airport. Not just propositioned. She'd provided the room and stripped naked in hopes he wouldn't walk out the door before he fucked her.

What were the odds she'd end up working in the town he lived in, or he'd fuck her over in a much more pleasant way than she'd fucked him?

She hadn't actually done anything to him back in New York, but she'd worked for one of the people who had screwed him over. She'd been screwed, too, in a manner of speaking. She'd followed her boss/boyfriend's orders like a good little minion, all the way up until the day he and his secret lover disappeared with most of William Ingram's money and all the paintings he'd entrusted them with for a gallery showing.

Cecil hadn't even liked Ingram's paintings, but the woman he'd run off with, Will's agent and girlfriend, Jessica, had done nothing but gush about how wonderful her client's work was. All while she had apparently been planning to end his career.

Kenzie had expected the paintings to start showing up on the black market, but it hadn't been the case. Months went by without a single one of them surfacing. There was no evidence they'd been destroyed.

Surely, they would have left the debris where it could be found. Wouldn't they? Why haul them off if you planned to destroy them?

It was all such a fucked-up mess, she couldn't wrap her head around it. All she knew for sure was one day she had a boyfriend, a job, and a place to live. And the next, she'd had none of those things. She'd been questioned by the police several times. Her life had been taken apart at the seams and haphazardly put back together. They found nothing because she knew nothing. She'd thought Cecil had been faithful, as she had, to their relationship. After going over every minute of the six months leading up to the heist and disappearance, she had come up with nothing. Not a single clue to what the pair had planned. They'd simply disappeared. Poof! Now you see them. Now you don't.

Kenzie blew out a frustrated breath, blinked back the tears threatening to spill over, and focused on her surroundings. Will Ingram was going to find out who she really was. In fact, she was surprised he hadn't put it together in his head already. MacKenzie wasn't a common name, and she was from New York. She hadn't even pretended not to know what had happened to him. Everyone in New York talked about nothing else for months. The story had been on all the local and national news stations and made the front page of every newspaper and news magazine there was. She'd only been referred to as Cecil's girlfriend and gallery employee in all the news reports. However, her full name was in the official police files multiple times. Surely, he'd seen it.

Well, she wasn't going to look a gift horse in the mouth. As long as he didn't know, she wasn't going to tell him.

Mel and Cathy would come searching for her soon. Pushing away from the wall, she hustled two doors down to the drugstore and walked the aisles. She didn't really need anything, but as she heard the bell over the front door jingle, and glanced over her shoulder to see her companions enter the store, she blindly grabbed a couple of items from the nearest shelf and made her way to the checkout. She dropped her purchases onto the counter and dug in her purse for her wallet as the older woman at the register began to ring up the sale.

"Think you're going to need all those?" Cathy's humor-laced question prompted Kenzie to examine the boxes she'd snatched from the aisle.

Oh, god! Her fingers tightened around the plastic card in her hand as a wave of embarrassment heated her skin.

On the counter sat three boxes of condoms and a tube of lube.

"Credit or debit?"

"Uh."

"The brothers Grim are made of granite, but not in a good way," Cathy said. "But good luck to you." She gestured to the counter. "I hope you need all those and more."

The cashier sighed and pointed to a card reader. "Slide it in the slot, or insert it if it has a chip."

Behind her, Mel and Cathy dissolved into a fit of giggles they did a poor job of hiding. There was only one way out of this mess. She turned the card to match the picture on the device and inserted it into the chip reader. She shook her head and, over her shoulder, commented, "Next time we need balloons for a bridal shower, the two of you have to buy them. I'm done." She smiled at the unforgiving face across the counter. The card reader beeped. She removed the card, held out her hand for her receipt as she snatched the bag containing her purchases. "Sorry about my friends. They're usually more mature."

"No problem," the woman said without cracking a smile. "Have fun at the shower."

Cathy bumped shoulders with Kenzie once they were out on the sidewalk again. "Are you going to tell us the real reason you just bought enough condoms to supply an entire football team after the homecoming dance?"

Kenzie sighed. "No. I'm not." Nothing she could make up would be any less embarrassing than the truth—she'd been thinking about Will

Ingram—and maybe, subconsciously, had ended up in that particular aisle.

"Leave her alone," Mel said. "It's none of our business. MacKenzie is a grown woman."

"Okay, okay," Cathy sulked. "But do me one favor?"

Kenzie glanced at her new friend.

"If you get the opportunity to use some of those, I'll need details."

Kenzie smiled. "Not unless you provide details first. Mel and I want to hear all about you and Rick."

They stopped in front of the hardware store, where Mel assured her they could find the paint she needed. Cathy paused with her hand on the old-fashioned doorknob. "Fine. But you're going to be disappointed."

"I seriously doubt it," Mel said and followed Cathy inside the store.

CATHY'S HOUSE REFLECTED the woman's personality with its cozy furniture and brightly colored accoutrements. Kenzie immediately felt at home, which was why she was in the kitchen, opening the bottle of wine she'd brought to share for their girls' night out while Mel and Cathy relaxed in the family room. She wasn't at all surprised when Mel's raised voice met her ears.

"Kenzie! When are we going to be able to invade your house?"

The two of them had been alternating between their houses for their biweekly evenings out and were "chomping at the bit," whatever *that* meant, to add her place to the rotation.

Strolling in, open bottle in hand, Kenzie refilled Cathy's glass then Mel's before pouring herself a generous amount. "I'm working on it." After settling in the big overstuffed chair across from the sofa where her friends sat, she took a sip from her glass. "Some of the furniture I ordered online is arriving later this week. I've got a few key pieces—a bed, a table and chairs in the kitchen, and a television. All the things Mel and I bought are supposed to arrive tomorrow. And don't forget, Rick Ingram is supposed to start the kitchen remodel next week. I have no idea how long it will take, but I'm thinking of asking him to paint some walls for me before he starts tearing things out."

"Rick is going to remodel your kitchen?" Cathy asked.

"So it seems." Kenzie wiggled to get more comfortable in the big chair. "He called me at the office yesterday. He's starting his own contracting business, and, apparently, I'm his first customer. Well, technically, Henry Travis is his customer. I'm just there to supervise and answer questions as they come up."

"I didn't know he was starting his own business." Cathy sipped from her glass. "Good for him."

Mel cradled her wineglass in both hands. "So, are you going to tell us what happened between you and Rick?"

Cathy gulped half the liquid in her glass then set it on the coffee table and tucked her legs underneath her. "Okay. I can see the two of you aren't going to let this go, so I'll tell you. Then I don't want to hear another thing about it. Are we clear?"

Mel and Kenzie both nodded. "Not another word," Kenzie said.

"What she said, now spill."

Cathy took a deep breath then let it out. "I've known the brothers all my life. This is a small town, was even smaller when we were kids. The Ingram's lived on the next street over—a few houses down from Hank. We all played together...rode our bikes all over the neighborhood...built lemonade stands together...roller-skated on the sidewalks. Stuff kids do.

"Then we grew up, and the boys started noticing other girls, except for Rick. He was my first date. We were thirteen."

"Thirteen?" Mel sat up straighter. "Kinda young, don't you think?"

"Maybe," Cathy conceded. "But my parents knew him and trusted him. He was a good kid. Didn't get into trouble."

"Go on," Kenzie urged. "Where did you go on your first date?"

"We walked into town—all of three blocks—to the soda fountain at Harrington's Pharmacy. I had a root beer float and he had a purple cow."

"Yuck!" Mel made a face. "A purple cow?"

"Yep. It was his favorite." Silence filled the air as Cathy decided on her next words. "As you can guess, there wasn't much for teenagers to do in Willowbrook back then. We spent a lot of time at the soda fountain, went to the movies, and studied together at the library. At least that was what we told our parents when we wanted to be alone."

"Where *did* you go?" Mel asked.

"There are some secluded places in the park. Make-out places. Rick had two older brothers, so he knew them all. Jake wouldn't take us anywhere, but when Will got his driver's license, he'd take us places. The drive-in was a favorite. We'd take the front seat so Will and his date could have the back."

Mel massaged her temples with the fingers of one hand while holding her wineglass with the other. "Geez, Cathy."

"Yeah, we were young. And stupid. I loved him, and he loved me." She grabbed her glass and drained it. Kenzie refilled it then sat back, waiting for the rest of the story. "We didn't go all the way until we were sixteen. It was his birthday and he'd just gotten his driver's license. Jake was away at college, and we took his old junker car to the drive-in. Rick said he loved me, and we'd already done everything except *you know*, so we did it in the back seat."

"How romantic." Kenzie shifted in her seat.

Cathy shrugged. "I said we were young and stupid."

"How was it?" Mel asked.

"Awkward. Beautiful. I loved him. Was glad to give him what he wanted. We were together for another year, screwing our brains out at every opportunity then we had a fight."

"Over what?"

"I thought I might be pregnant. We were careful—always used protection. Remember, Rick has older brothers. Four males living in one house. I suspect they bought condoms by the case. Anyway, I was late and I told Rick. He went ballistic. We broke up for a while." Cathy looked at Mel. "That's when I dated Hank. I was still in love with Rick and Hank knew it, I suspect. At any rate, Rick and I got back together before our senior year. I knew he wanted to go into the military, but I never thought he would actually do it. He had the grades to get into any college he wanted. He went off the rails a bit the year his mom died, but he was a straight-A student the rest of the time. I underestimated how badly Rick wanted out of Willowbrook, I guess. He enlisted in the Marines the day before graduation. I was going to junior college, and he was going god knew where."

"I'm so sorry." Mel set her glass on the coffee table then scooted down the sofa to hug Cathy.

When they parted, Cathy continued, "He said he loved me but he had to go. It wasn't me; it was him. Yada, yada. I'd been a fool. I gave Rick everything, thinking we'd be together forever, but he discarded me like I was no more important than those stupid paper caps and gowns we wore for graduation."

Kenzie grabbed a tissue box from the end table and handed it to her crying hostess. She was getting a clearer picture of what had happened, though she felt there were still pieces of the puzzle missing. Cathy had been dreaming of marriage and white picket fences while Rick had been dreaming of escape. From what, was the question. "He didn't write or call?"

Cathy shook her head and yanked a couple of tissues from the box. "No."

"Have you spoken to him since he came home?"

"No."

"Maybe he's waiting for you to make the first move?"

Cathy's grunt said it all. "He'll be waiting until Hell freezes over."

Mel picked up the bottle and refilled her glass. "Are you still in love with him?"

"No! God, no." Cathy blew her nose, clutching the used tissues in a tight fist. "He's obviously not the same person he was in high school."

"Are you the same person you were then?" Kenzie asked.

Cathy sipped from her glass. "I don't suppose I am."

"Maybe you should contact him," Mel said, settling against the arm of the sofa. "It's been a long time. I bet he doesn't know how to approach you."

Their friend drained her glass, refilled it from the rapidly emptying bottle, and sat back.

"What do you know about Will?" Kenzie asked.

"I think I told you all I know. He went to New York to study art—against his father's wishes, as I recall. Rick and I were done shortly after Will left town. I have no idea what happened to make him as grim as his brothers."

Kenzie knew, but she had no intention of telling anyone. It had all been big news in New York, but not so much here, she thought. She would have expected everyone in Will's hometown to have followed his career, but it didn't seem to be the case. Maybe that was why he came back here instead of staying in New York. She could sure relate to the need for a change, and Willowbrook was as different from the Big Apple as any place could be.

"I wonder if he's here to stay?" Mel set her glass on the coffee table. "Hank and his other friends would like it if he stayed."

"That group was thick as thieves," Cathy said. "Hank, Will, Randy, and Chris."

"Who are Randy and Chris?" Kenzie couldn't recall hearing them mentioned before.

"You'll meet Randy soon enough. He's the only other lawyer in town, and he handles all Hank's legal stuff. Chris runs the farm for

Hank as well as his own family's farm. He's a busy guy, but you'll probably see him around from time to time."

"I wondered who was taking care of the crops. It looks like a big responsibility."

Mel stretched her legs out straight and wiggled her bare toes. "Hank helps when he can, but he can't count on being around when things need to get done, so it's easier to put Chris in charge. At least he knows what he's doing. Can't say Hank does."

"Guess he can't be good at everything." Kenzie carried her glass to the kitchen. "I better get home," she said as she slipped her sandals back on her feet for the walk home. "Tomorrow's a big day—my busiest yet at BlackWing."

"Really?" Mel stood, too. "What's going on?"

"I've arranged a bunch of remote radio interviews for Hank. We'll be in the studio for most of the day answering the same boring questions for talk show hosts across the country."

She wasn't looking forward to the long day, but as Hank said, it beat the heck out of traveling to all those cities for five minutes of work.

"He mentioned you'd set those up. I can't tell you how happy he was you'd arranged it so he could stay home. He really does hate to travel, especially when it doesn't include a performance."

"I'm working on some of those, too. If all goes as planned, Black-Wing will be one of the featured performers for the morning show's concert in the park series later this year."

"Oh. My. God. Seriously?" Mel bounced on the balls of her feet. "The guys will bust a gut! They've wanted to be a part of that series for years."

"Well, don't get their hopes up too high. I'm still negotiating with the network and the show's producers. There's lots of competition and only so many Fridays in the summer." It would be a huge accomplishment if she scored them a spot on the roster. Lucky for her, an old friend from her days at NYU worked in the network's offices now and had a bit of pull when it came to booking the slots. She was going to owe Avery big-time if BlackWing made the list.

Kenzie was glad she'd decided to walk the few blocks from her house to Cathy's. Used to walking everywhere in New York, she missed the daily exercise. Maybe she'd have to take up running to keep the pounds off. As far as she could tell, salad was something Texans fed to rabbits. When she did find it on a menu, it was topped with fried chicken or steak and smothered in a creamy dressing. Neither was doing anything for her figure—except making it expand.

CHAPTER EIGHT

The night air felt good on her skin, and the moonlight playing peek-a-boo through the leaves of the trees lining the street was more than enough to show the way. The occasional porch light left on provided additional illumination.

Kenzie turned the corner onto her street and stopped beneath the streetlamp to admire the tranquil scene. Old-growth trees between the street and sidewalk acted as sentinels at night and provided shade during the day. Other than a car passing now and then, there was no traffic to speak of. Insects she couldn't identify provided a nocturnal symphony she'd come to appreciate in the absence of city noise. Treading the uneven walkway at a pace that would get her runover in New York, she let her mind wander to the one subject she couldn't seem to eradicate from her mind—William Ingram.

Having the memory of their close encounter in the Philly airport was bad enough, but now she had the memory of him in front of the hardware store, so close his unique scent swirled around her, through her. So close she could feel the heat radiating off his body. So close she could see the depth of pain in his dark eyes. So close all she had to do was reach out to touch him. But she hadn't. Couldn't. He wasn't an anonymous hookup in an airport any longer. He was W. H. Ingram. A man she couldn't have, no matter what her traitorous body said.

She'd felt sorry for him when everything hit the fan back in New York, but since she'd seen the pain etched deep on his face and swirling in his eyes, guilt for the small part she'd played in his demise ate at her.

The pain had been there in Philly. Maybe it was what drew her to him in the first place. Misery loves company. Had she known who he was then, she wouldn't have gone anywhere near him. But she hadn't known, and when her pain had collided with his, they'd combusted. Sparks had flown. It was a wonder they hadn't burned the place down.

Sex had never been stupendous for her. Good, yes. Good enough she hadn't wanted to give it up, but since their encounter in Philly, she *craved* it. Not just any sex. She wanted more of what she'd had with Hot Guy, a.k.a. W.H. Ingram.

Only it wasn't going to happen. He'd made it perfectly clear the other day he wanted nothing to do with her. *Yeah, he'd want even less to do with you if he knew who you really were.*

If she had any brains at all, she'd get the heck out of Willowbrook before he found out. People in this town loved him. They didn't know her. She'd lose any popularity contest between them.

Lost in thought, she jumped when a shadowy figure moved on a nearby porch. Hand on her throat, she took a step back before she realized this was Willowbrook not New York. It was one of her neighbors in a town where a rash of toilet-papered trees constituted a crime spree.

"Didn't mean to startle you."

She recognized his voice. Her heart raced. She'd been wrong. So very wrong. This man was dangerous in so many ways. Yet, instead of running toward the safety of her new home, her feet remained planted on the sidewalk, as the figure stepped from the shadows.

"Out a little late, aren't you?"

"What are you? My mother?"

"Nope. Just a concerned citizen looking out for the welfare of our newest resident."

"It's none of your business, but I was at a friend's house."

"Did you have a nice time at Cathy's?"

"How?" she squeaked as her mind raced to figure out how he'd known where she was. "Are you following me?"

"Nope." He tapped his temple. "I have excellent powers of deduction. You're new to town, and I doubt you've had time to make many friends. You know Cathy. I saw you with her at the diner, remember? She lives on the next street over. Thus, it's logical to deduce you were at her place."

She latched on to the subject like it was a lifeline. Anything to keep from doing what she really wanted to do—drag him into the bushes for a repeat. "You know Cathy?"

He strolled closer, hands stuffed in the front pockets of his jeans. "Yep. All my life."

"That's...uh...nice." Damn, why couldn't she string two words together without stumbling over them? Maybe it was because of the way he was looking at her. Suddenly, she felt like the adult version of Red Riding Hood. And W.H. Ingram was her personal big, bad wolf. The feeble grandma in the deepest recesses of her brain urged her to run, but her overactive libido wouldn't let her move.

"She mentioned you the other day when I went in to pick up some donuts. She seemed glad to have you here."

It was good to know she was making friends in Willowbrook, but there was someone else's opinion she was more interested in. "And what about you?"

He drew closer and leaned against the corner post of the white picket fence surrounding his yard. "I hate having you in the same town."

"Oh. Well." She looked down at her feet and silently willed them to move.

"I hate that I want you even more than the first time I saw you."

Kenzie jerked her chin up. "What?"

"I said, I hate that I still want you." His gaze swept the surrounding area then landed on hers. "I can't stop thinking about you—or all the things I want to do to you."

"L-like what?"

"For starters, I want to turn your naked ass over my knee and spank you until your skin is red and your pussy is dripping wet. Then I want to fuck you six ways to Sunday." He paused, shook his head as if to clear it then his gaze met hers again. "I don't want a relationship. Just sex. Raw. Nasty. Sex."

She forced air into her lungs, struggling to comprehend his words. "You up for a purely physical arrangement, Kenzie?"

LORD, WHEN DID I BECOME such a prick?

Will knew the answer to the question but refused to think about it right then. MacKenzie was from New York. She understood the game. She'd proven it when she propositioned him in the airport. He'd been a prick then, too, but she'd gotten what she'd asked for. Since he was doing the propositioning, he hoped she didn't expect anything more than what he'd given her in their rented room. If she did, she was in for a rude awakening. *If* she said yes. And that was a big if.

Against his conscious will, he committed her shocked face to memory, filing the image away with the others he couldn't seem to get out of his head. In the dark of night, they came to him, waking him from what little sleep he got these days, torturing him, tormenting him until he did something about the fire raging inside him. He was damn sick of his right hand. Had even tried to do it left-handed just to mix things up a bit.

He hadn't considered propositioning her until he'd seen her turn the corner a few houses down and felt his body come alive with need. Willowbrook had grown some since he'd been gone. He could probably find companionship somewhere else if he wanted to, but he didn't want anyone else. For whatever reason, it was this woman, and only her, who stirred his cock to life.

She closed her mouth, glanced around him to the porch where he'd been sitting, contemplating the next chapter of his life. "Where?"

WILL

Every nerve ending in his body stood up and took notice. *Holy crap!* He should have thought this through, but he'd been certain she would say no. What were his options? The house was out. Rick was home, and there was nothing but a thin wall between the two bedrooms. There was the garage...fuck, no. He wasn't *that* desperate. *Think. Think.*

"My place." Her fingers closed around his right wrist, dragging his hand from his pocket as she started walking. "Hurry the fuck up."

Yes, ma'am!

The walk was painful as hell. He'd been hard since the moment he laid eyes on her, but that one little word from her lips—"Where?"—and he'd gone hard as stone. He knew the street well. Knew every crack in the sidewalk, every house and its inhabitants. Not much had changed in the years he'd been gone.

"Careful," he said, lacing his fingers with hers to guide her over a spot where tree roots had raised the walkway, leaving a crack wide enough to catch a foot.

"Thanks." She squeezed his hand then pulled hers free.

They turned up the walk leading to her front door. Will blocked out the memory of this being Hank's house—a place he'd spent many a day and night—and concentrated on the woman opening the front door. He didn't want to take his eyes off of her, but the minute he stepped inside, a wave of nostalgia swept over him. The living room was empty except for a new sofa and a flat-screen television resting on the floor. He could still see the furniture Hank's mom, Gloria, had taken such pride in—and the easy chair his dad, Henry, had claimed as his own. Blinking, he forced the memories away. The previous occupants of the house had moved on, and so had he. The house down the street where he'd grown up wasn't home any more, either.

"Sorry. I don't have much furniture yet."

"No problem. We don't need much." He strode toward the kitchen, hoping she at least had the basics in there. He wasn't disappointed. A small table sat in the exact same spot as the one he remembered. He pulled out a chair, turned it around, and sat. "This will do fine."

"You want to do it in here?"

"You have a problem with kitchen sex?"

"No." Her brows knit. "I have a bed."

"Don't need one." He made himself comfortable on the chair. "Come here."

She approached, one cautious step at a time. He pointed to a spot beside his right thigh and saw the moment comprehension dawned on her expressive face. In the span of a second, she went from confused to aroused as she relocated to the spot he'd indicated.

"Push your pants and panties to your knees then lay across my lap."

With a slight nod, she eased shaking hands beneath her loose pullover top to the waistband of her yoga pants. Will swallowed hard as she wiggled out of the tight garment, her oversized shirt falling to cover much of her exposed skin. No matter. He had a vivid memory. An artist's memory. He could still recall the gentle swell of her belly and the neatly trimmed curls on the crest of her womanhood.

"Help me?"

He jerked his attention to the present and the bare thighs pressed against his denim-clad leg. "Put your hands behind you and bend over. I won't let you fall."

God, he was going to die right here if he didn't get his heart rate under control. The damn organ was working overtime to pump blood to his dick. He needed a little of it to remain above his neck long enough for him to get through this portion of the night's entertainment without actually hurting her. Yes, he was going to spank the hell out of her ass, but he wouldn't cause actual harm. No way. Not his style.

He eased her into place then brushed the hem of her shirt up to the small of her back before he clamped her wrists in his left hand. "Don't want you to get hurt," he explained. "If you want me to stop, say red.

If you need a break, say yellow. Otherwise, I'm in control here. Understood?"

"Yes."

"So we're clear, this spanking is not a punishment. It's because I can't get you out of my head." Yeah, the statement didn't even make sense to him, but he wasn't going to stop unless she put the brakes on. He'd honor her wishes, but, judging from the heightened scent of her arousal, she wanted this as much as he did. "Tell me you understand. Tell me you want me to spank you."

"I want this. Please, spank me."

Without warning, he brought his palm down hard on her right ass cheek, leaving a clear imprint. She cried out, but her cry quickly morphed into a groan. Shit, she was going to be the death of him.

He repeated the process on her left cheek then gently massaged the twin red handprints until she was groaning and writhing on his lap. "God, I love seeing my mark on you." He squeezed the plump globes before stroking them again, firm but soft. "I wanted to leave my mark on you before—"

He landed two more strikes slightly off center from the others. Her skin flamed red where the two overlapped. Christ, he wanted to paint her like this. His stupid brain was already mixing colors to achieve the perfect shade. Angry with himself, he landed four more blows, not as hard as before—he didn't dare in his state of mind—but hard enough to have her trying to jerk out of his grasp.

Breathing hard, he laid his palm on her ass. "Too much?"

"No."

He could hear the tears in her voice and instantly felt like a shit. "Want me to stop? Just say the word."

"Please, Will. I need—"

"What, baby?" He knew, but the perverse person he was, he wanted to hear her say it. To beg for it.

"I need to come. Please, Will."

He parted her ass cheeks with his middle finger, sliding lower until he found her drenched center. Her pants, bunched at her knees, held her legs together, and though he would have loved to have been able to see more, the position was good for her. Her thighs held him snug as he pushed two fingers inside her tight entrance then found her clit with his little finger. "You want it, baby? Ride my hand. Make it happen."

God, I really am a bastard. But, Heaven help him, watching her ass buck and wiggle, hearing her cries of frustration as she sought the release she so desperately needed was possibly the most erotic thing he'd ever witnessed in his life. "That's it, baby. Make yourself come then I'm going to fuck you so hard. I'm going to ram my cock in you over and over. Take what I want and leave you wet and sore."

"Fuck. You!" Her body tensed. He smiled as she screamed out her pleasure. He'd been right not to take her to his house. They'd be lucky if her neighbors didn't call the cops.

He released her wrists then stroked her ass and beneath her shirt as far as he could easily reach until her breathing evened out and she tried to sit up.

"Fuck you, Will Ingram." The weak smile on her flushed face made a lie out of her curse.

"You're welcome." He stood. "My turn now." He held out a hand to help her stand. "Kick those pants off and grip the edge of the table. You know the drill."

Legs still trembling from one of the most intense orgasms she'd ever had, Kenzie did as Will said so she stood before him naked from the waist down. Following the silent signal of his spinning index finger, she turned and stretched over the table, gripping the far edge with her fingers. The cold wood on her heated skin was a shock to her senses. Pain from pressing her breasts, tight with arousal, against the table was an unexpected aphrodisiac. Without being told, she spread her feet wide, presenting her pussy to him. How was it possible she still needed to feel him inside her, stretching her, filling her? She'd had enough solo orgasms to know once was usually enough, but not with him.

She'd wanted him again at the airport, and nothing had changed. She still wanted him. Feared she'd always want him. But from the position he'd chosen, then and now, he didn't want more. Just a hard fuck. A release.

No kissing. No tender caresses, unless you could count the way he'd massaged the sting of his handprints into a slow burn that had ignited a conflagration within. Those gentle touches had been a surprise, but as she listened to the sound of a zipper being lowered and plastic ripping, she understood there'd be no conciliatory gestures this time.

Internal muscles clamped tight then released. She was wet in anticipation of his entry.

"Red is your only word; otherwise, I'm not stopping until I'm finished. Come if you want to. Won't make a difference to me." He drew the head of his cock along her slit then fitted himself to her opening and dug his fingers into her hips. "Tell me you want me to fuck you."

Hell, yes! "Please, fuck me, Will. Fuck me hard."

His first hard thrust rocked her pelvis against the edge of the table and drove her lungs up into her throat. She gasped for air and held on for what she was certain would be the ride of her life.

She wasn't disappointed. His cock was every bit as big and hard as she remembered, his grip as tight, his stamina impressive. She was going to be sore tomorrow in places she'd never been sore before, but she wouldn't stop him. It felt too damn good. He took and took and took, and god, it felt glorious to be the one he lost control with. Kenzie gave and gave and gave, but it wasn't unselfish. He took his pleasure, and in doing so, gave her more.

"Ride the edge of the table. Fuck it, baby."

God, she loved his dirty talk. She groaned and moved her hips as best she could, grinding her clit against the unforgiving wood while Will continued to pound his pelvis against the abused flesh of her ass.

He eased his grip on her hips, allowing her more movement. She rode toward her release, felt the coil inside her tightening. Then he slipped a thumb between her cheeks, found her most secret place, and pushed brutally inside.

Pain and embarrassment melded into a solid wedge jettisoning her into a place she'd never been before where pleasure and pain were one and the same. A place where the thick cock pummeling was all she needed. All she wanted. She convulsed, over and over again, clamping down on his shaft, and she knew, in an instant of clarity and awareness, this man had been made for her. There would be no other. Ever.

"Fuck me! You feel good." His curses made their way past the blood rushing in her ears. "God, woman, you're killing me."

Kenzie found the willpower to order her internal muscles to grip him tight one more time. Her effort was rewarded as his thrusts became erratic and his curses garbled. Then, with a series of short, brutal thrusts, he came, his dick pulsing inside her, filling the condom and making her heart ache, wanting to feel his hot seed bathe her inner walls, knowing she never would. Tears spilled from her eyes. Tears of regret for what they could never have together. He didn't know who she really was. Didn't know what part she'd played in his downfall. He would find out, and when he did, all she'd have left would be the memory of these perfect moments when they'd shared an intimacy, a bond beyond the physical.

It was impossible, but her heart belonged to W.H. Ingram.

CHAPTER NINE

I'm an ass.

Hands tucked into his front pockets, shoulders slumped, Will's feet carried him down Main Street to the park where he'd be alone at this time of night. He'd done it again, fucked her then left without a word.

Shit.

He'd never been a coward before, but he was now. How else could he explain his behavior? Fuckin' afraid to look her in the eye. What was with him?

He knew. It was the pain he'd seen in those eyes—twice. Once when she sat down next to him in the airport bar then just the other day when he'd confronted her outside the diner. She hurt inside just like he did. If he hung around, inevitably, they'd talk. It was how relationships worked. The last thing he wanted to do was share his pain with anyone. The humiliation went too deep, the wound too fresh. And if he was being truthful, he flat out didn't want to carry anyone else's burden. His was heavy enough.

Yep. A cowardly ass. That's me.

This can't go on.

But as long as he continued to feel like a victim, he'd never have a chance at a normal relationship again. Hell, he didn't have a chance at a normal life of any kind. It was time to get his shit together. Time to own his circumstances. Time to fight. Maybe, if he knew he'd done everything he could to get his paintings back—never mind the money—he'd be able to move forward.

He wanted to paint. He just couldn't see the point in it anymore. The situation had to change because, without his paints, he didn't know who he was.

And not knowing fucking sucked.

JAKE OPENED HIS FRONT door, wearing sweatpants bearing the Yale logo and a T-shirt Will suspected dated to his brother's days as quarterback for the Willowbrook Wildcats. Though it was late, he didn't look at all surprised to see Will on his doorstep. "It's about time."

Refusing to be baited, Will pushed past him in the entryway of the ultra-modern home his brother had built on the outskirts of town and marched straight for the kitchen where he'd find a cold beer in the refrigerator. He might need something more bracing before this conversation was over, but, for now, a beer would do. He popped a top on one, handed it to Jake who'd followed him through the house then opened one for himself. He closed the refrigerator and leaned against the fancy quartz countertop. "The last thing I want to do is talk about this, but I need help."

Jake opened his mouth to say something, but Will cut him off.

"Don't say it, Jake. I know I've been a jerk. I should have asked for your help months ago, but I didn't. Can't change the past. I'm here now. That should count for something."

Jake nodded and took a sip of his drink. "I was going to ask if you would like to sit down." He pointed with the hand holding the bottle. "Den or out by the pool?"

"Pool." Will followed his brother who stopped in his home office to grab a yellow pad and a pen before proceeding to the back of the house where an expansive patio looked out on a vanishing-edge pool and several acres of lakefront property. Jake wouldn't have suggested they talk outdoors if he thought there was a chance in hell someone would overhear. He hadn't gotten to be the successful attorney he was by doing stupid things.

Will, too agitated to completely relax, straddled a lounge chair, while his brother stretched out on the adjacent chaise. Between the underwater lighting and a nearby lamppost, there was just enough light for Jake to take notes. Though the setting was casual, Will sensed his brother slip into lawyer mode—silent and predatory. He'd hear every word Will had to say and note every word he didn't say. There'd be no hiding from the truth tonight.

Will took a long pull on his beer then, gaze focused on the dark horizon, told his story. Starting from the moment he'd met his agent, Jessica Blackwell, to the evening he'd shown up at Cecil Hawthorne's gallery to find the doors locked and his paintings gone. He left nothing out, including the fact he'd been sleeping with Jessica since he'd met her at another opening, also held at Hawthorne's gallery.

The more he talked, the stupider he sounded. He'd been in love, or so he thought, but in retrospect, his relationship with Jess had been a sham from the outset.

"You think they targeted you from the beginning?"

Leave it to Jake to get right to the heart of the matter. "I think it's possible. I didn't then. Never saw it coming. I thought we were in love. We made plans." Plans he didn't want to think about ever again. He'd given his heart to a thief and wouldn't make the same mistake again.

"What kind of plans? Was anything in writing? Did you buy property together?"

Will shook his head. "No. Nothing like that. We talked about buying a place upstate. Something with an outbuilding I could use as a studio. Even rented a car and took a few trips up there to scout areas."

"Did you talk to a real estate agent?"

"Once. We stopped to eat at a local diner. The agent was next door. Had some flyers in the window. One of them looked promising, so we went in to ask about it."

"Did you go look at the property?"

"No. It had already been sold. He just hadn't taken the flyers down."

Jake scribbled furiously on his pad. "Tell me everything you remember about the visit."

"Why? We didn't do anything but talk to the guy."

"Humor me, okay?"

Will sat up, his legs splayed on either side of the lounger. Shoulders slumped, he bowed his head and closed his eyes, searching for memories he'd tried desperately to erase from his mind. He couldn't imagine any of this would matter, but he trusted Jake. If anyone could find a thread to pull in this case, it was his brother. "We'd been together for almost a year," he began.

Even the crickets had called it a night by the time Jake finished his interrogation. They'd been down roads Will hadn't dared explore and through doors he hadn't even known were there. His brother was good. Really good. Though he was rung out from all the talking and soul-baring, he felt better for having told his story to someone who really listened. The police had heard him out, but he never felt as if they'd listened.

Jake returned from the house with two cups of coffee and a plastic bag. He set the cups of steaming liquid on the small table between them then set about filling the bag with empty beer bottles. They'd consumed more than Will realized over the last few hours.

"Thanks." He picked up one of the mugs.

"You should spend what's left of the night here."

Will nodded. "Might be a good idea. I'll call Rick." After leaving the park, he'd gone home and helped himself to his younger brother's pickup. "Let him know I'll bring his truck back early."

"I called him. He said if you weren't back in time, he'd walk down to Henry's house in the morning. It's just a walk-through with the new tenant to get a feel for what has to be done and establish a schedule."

Mention of Henry Travis' new tenant did more than any cup of coffee could do to sober him up. He stifled a groan as he recalled the way he'd treated her. Getting to his feet, he followed his brother inside the house. He'd been there enough times to know his way around. The common rooms, kitchen, living room, and den were in the center of the sprawling ranch-style structure. The master suite and Jake's office took up one end of the house. Will sauntered in the opposite direction, toward a selection of guest rooms to choose from.

"Wait a second." Jake disappeared into his office. A few seconds later, he emerged with a yellow tablet and pen in hand. "Here. Take these. If you remember anything at all, write it down. And when I say anything, I mean even the smallest detail. Even if you don't think it's significant." Jake grinned. "You never know. It could be the key we're looking for."

Will nodded. Just as he'd taken another step, Jake's voice stopped him again. "Oh, and I need a list of every gallery where your paintings were sold. Names, addresses, any—"

"Anything. I get it." He waved the pad of paper in a goodnight gesture then resumed walking. He'd been looking forward to a good night's sleep, unburdened as he was after spilling his guts to his brother, but Jake's last comments had jump-started his brain again. There'd be precious little sleep, if any, tonight.

CHAPTER TEN

Kenzie placed her palms flat on the table and pushed herself upright. Her knees buckled under her weight, and she grabbed for the nearest chair, the one Will had sat in only a few minutes ago, and crumpled onto the seat, the sound of his footsteps walking away still echoing in her ears.

Hell and damnation. He'd told her up front what he wanted. Raw, nasty sex. And he'd delivered. Nothing more.

So, why did her heart hurt so damn bad?

You knew the score. You agreed to his terms.

At least she was pretty sure the airport encounter hadn't been a revenge fuck as she'd thought. Those were a one-and-done. He'd come back for more—admitted he wanted her—but wished he didn't.

Welcome to the crowd.

She needed to stay far away from Will Ingram. Far. Far. Away. He'd eventually find out who she was. He apparently hadn't linked her name to his scandal yet, but he would. And when he did, god help her. He'd destroy her.

She hated he held that kind of power over her, but there wasn't a thing she could do about it. If only she'd met him in New York before things had gotten so screwed up. Maybe things would have been different for both of them. Would he have given her a second look back then? Probably not. According to the news reports, he'd been involved with his agent up until the night Jessica and Cecil betrayed him.

Had he been in love with her? Was losing her more of a blow than the loss of his money and paintings? Was lost love the pain she saw in his eyes?

She didn't want to think what a lost love, if it was true, made her relationship with Will.

Whoa! Hold the fuck right up! There is no relationship. None. Nada. Zip.

They were....

Absolutely nothing came to mind. Not friends with benefits. Not fuck buddies, but not exactly enemies, either. Though they would be as soon as he realized who she was.

Kenzie closed her eyes and did the deep breathing exercises she'd learned during her short stint in a yoga class a few years ago. She'd been horrible at the exercises, but she'd found the breathing techniques useful on occasion. Tonight was no exception. After a few minutes, her heart rate calmed and her mind cleared enough for her to take stock of her circumstances.

Her ass hurt sitting on the hard wooden chair. The sensations coming from between her legs were a mix of satisfaction and a hollow ache tied to her heart with invisible strings. With effort she found hard to come by, she rose, picked up the small pile of her clothes, and trudged to her bedroom.

Not even a hot bath had eased the ache between her legs, so she'd tossed and turned most of the night, determined not to give in to the need to touch herself. The few minutes she'd slept, she hadn't been alone. Will Ingram had invaded her dreams, fulfilling them one second then dissolving into nightmares the next when her truth came to light.

Groaning, she dropped her forehead into one upturned palm while the other held tight to the mug of hot caffeine she hoped would obliterate last night from her memories—if she could find the energy to lift the cup to her lips and drink. Every muscle in her body ached. Some from the vigorous workout they'd had right there on her kitchen table, and others from a night fraught with tension, both real and imagined.

She'd taken a few hours off this morning to meet with the contractor Mr. Travis had hired to do the kitchen remodel. He'd be here any minute with plans and schedules.

Kenzie was pouring herself a second cup of coffee when the doorbell rang. Setting the mug aside, she took a deep breath and double-checked to make sure she'd actually dressed this morning. Any and everything was in question, given the state of her mind and body. Assured she'd put on clean clothes and was indeed presentable, she opened the front door—and gasped at the two men standing on her porch.

"MacKenzie Carlysle? I'm Rick Ingram. He hitched a thumb over his shoulder. And this is my brother, Will."

Shit. Shit. Shit. What was *he* doing here? Her hands clenched into fists, her nails digging painfully into her flesh as she stared at W.H. Ingram. His lips rose on one corner as he wiggled his fingers in a half-hearted wave. She wasn't sure which it was, the almost smile or the sight of his fingers doing *that*, that made her insides turn to liquid.

Rick held up a notebook. "We're here to go over the plans for the kitchen remodel. Mr. Travis has authorized a few more items he'd like done."

There was no hope for it, she had to let them in or try explaining why she didn't want Will Ingram in her house. She unlatched the screened door, giving it a slight push toward the two men. Rick grabbed the handle and stepped inside with his brother on his heels.

"Nice to meet you," Will said as if he hadn't ever seen her before.

Were they going to pretend they hadn't talked in front of the diner? Or had sex in her kitchen a few short hours ago? Apparently so. "Uh. Yeah. I mean, yes. It's nice to meet you, too." She turned, as much to avoid looking at him as to decide what to do with the two of them.

"Won't you have a seat?" She motioned to the lone sofa in the front room.

"Perhaps the kitchen would be a better place to talk," Rick said, "since the bulk of the work will be in there."

The kitchen. Visions of what had gone on in there less than twelve hours ago flashed through her brain. "Ri-right." It made sense. It did. But dear god, why did *he* have to be here? Calling upon every bit of manners she'd ever possessed, she led the way to the rear of the house. "I've got coffee—"

"Coffee would be great," Rick said, pulling out a chair at the table. Thank god it wasn't *the* chair. Kenzie found a couple of mugs her landlord had left and filled them. Turning around, she almost dropped them when she saw Will Ingram's hand on the back of a chair. The one he'd sat in the night before. The one she'd planted her bare ass on as he'd closed the front door, leaving her well fucked and more confused than she'd ever been in her life.

"Here. I'll take those." Will took the mugs from her and set them on the table. "Why don't you sit here so you can see the plans?" He indicated *the* chair without any hint it meant anything to him.

"Th-thanks." *Crap.* She really had to stop stammering. She sounded like an idiot. *Get a grip.*

What is he doing here?

"Is this yours?" He set the cup she'd abandoned earlier in front of her.

"Yes. Thank you." She gripped it with both hands like it was an anchor.

"My pleasure," he said as he slid into the chair on the other side of his brother.

She'd fire Rick if she could, but she wasn't the one paying him. Her landlord was. In exchange for overseeing the remodel, she was getting a significant discount on her rent until the project was done. She had no choice but to see this through, which meant she'd have to put on her big girl panties and deal.

Crap. She glanced at the floor where she'd dropped her panties last night so *her contractor's* brother could screw her brains out right here on the kitchen table. The tiny hairs on the back of her neck tingled like she was having an orgasm or someone was watching her. Absolutely certain it was the latter, she glanced up. Across the table where Rick was busy sorting papers for her to look at, her gaze met *his*. There wasn't a doubt in her mind he was thinking about last night, too.

Was that a smirk?

W.H. Ingram had a reputation for being arrogant, sometimes to the point of rudeness. He'd been famous for it in the New York art world. He didn't attend parties—just the occasional gallery showing for a friend. The magazine article and cover photo had been an anomaly, and had launched his fledgling career into the stratosphere where it had stayed until earlier this year.

He understood exactly what he did to her, and had done to her. How dare he sit there with a silly smirk on his face? Because he'd been inside her twice, he thought he had the upper hand. Thought he knew what she liked. He wasn't exactly wrong, but he didn't know everything. She liked a bit of cuddling after, but she'd never have that level of intimacy with Will. A bit of touch and kiss and maybe, if both parties weren't dead, another round—slower, with more feeling.

Shit. There she went again, hoping for something she would never find with Will Ingram. He didn't do relationships. He'd said so in plain English, and she'd acknowledged such. Kenzie squared her shoulders and dropped her gaze to a drawing Rick had placed in front of her. She didn't know what game Will was playing, but she was through.

"What's this?" She pointed to a big square on the meticulous layout.

"The refrigerator." Rick nodded toward the current one. "Mr. Travis agreed to a set amount to replace all the appliances. The one you have isn't too old. If you want, we can move it to the garage and you can continue to use it as an extra."

"Whatever would I need an extra refrigerator for?"

Rick shrugged. "Some people like to have them for overflow during the holidays. These kitchens are too small for a wine fridge, so you could fill it with your extra beverages."

"Did Mr. Travis want to keep it? Because I don't think I'll need it."

"Nope. He said to leave it up to you." Rick wrote something in his notebook. "Okay. I'll leave this one in place as long as possible then move it out to the garage until we're done. I'll have the delivery people haul it off when they bring the new appliances. Don't worry. I'll give you plenty of notice so you can get your stuff out."

"Oh. Thank you."

Rick was nice. The exact opposite of his brother who continued to stare at her while Rick walked her through his proposed timeline.

"That's about it," he said, "except for deciding on paint colors."

"Paint colors?"

"Mr. Travis authorized us to paint the interior and exterior of the house. White for the outside, but he said you could do whatever you wanted, within reason, inside."

"Mr. Travis is being exceptionally nice, but I can do the painting myself."

"Why would you want to?"

Truth was, she didn't know squat about painting, but she could learn. Mel and Cathy had promised to help when they'd taken her shopping for color swatches. "Won't interior painting slow down your remodel schedule?"

"Nope. Not a bit. Will has agreed to help me out. He'll do the outside while I'm demo-ing the old kitchen. As soon as he's finished outside, he'll get to work on the inside. All you have to do is choose the colors."

W.H. Ingram was going to paint her house. Paint. Her. House. "But—"

"Don't worry. He knows his way around a paintbrush. In fact, he just finished painting the outside of our house."

It was so absurd it was almost laughable. Kenzie choked back a nervous laugh. Did Rick not know? Of course he did, but for whatever reason, he was trying to protect his brother. If only he knew his brother didn't need protecting. W.H. Ingram could take care of himself. She turned her attention to her new paint contractor. "When can you get started, Mr. Ingram?"

"Tomorrow? I need to pick up paint and supplies today for the outside. Do you have any idea what color you want to paint the inside?"

Cathy had done a fantastic job of selecting colors for her, but W.H. Ingram didn't have to know she'd already made her decisions. She had a pretty good idea what his game was now. She made a snap decision to play along. "Nope. Why don't you pick up some paint chips while you're getting the things for the outside? Maybe you could bring them by this evening?"

Yep. He'd been waiting for her to issue an invitation. His lips lifted on one corner in a satisfied smirk. *Fuck you, Will Ingram.*

"Around seven?"

"Perfect." She'd have almost ten hours to find her dignity and the backbone she'd need to tell him his game was over. No matter how much she wanted him in her bed, or anywhere else, she needed to put an end to whatever it was they were doing. To continue on their present road would lead to nothing but heartache for her. Him? She was nothing but a warm body to him. She'd proven twice to be an easy conquest, so he had no reason to expect her to turn him down now.

CHAPTER ELEVEN

This is such a fuckin' bad idea.

The thought didn't stop Will from putting on a clean shirt, checking to make sure he had a condom tucked into his wallet, and walking down the sidewalk to what had once been the home of one of his best friends. Knowing a woman he had no reason to trust now lived there should have stopped him. But it didn't.

He couldn't get MacKenzie out of his head. She haunted his dreams and crept into his thoughts throughout the day. He wanted her—the physical desire being something of a miracle in itself. But it was more than physical desire. For the few minutes he'd been with her, he'd forgotten the shit-storm his life had become. He'd felt like a man in charge of his kingdom—something he hadn't experienced in a very long time. Truth be told, he'd lost his edge even before his career had come tumbling down around him.

Looking back, he should have realized how wrong his relationship with Jessica had been. The desire he'd felt for her at first had diminished a little more each time they'd been together, until it had all but disappeared, leaving an empty shell of a relationship. The last few months they'd been together, he hadn't touched her and she hadn't pushed for more. She'd turned to Cecil Hawthorne by then. Or had they been together all along?

This thing with MacKenzie felt different than any other relationship he'd ever been in. He'd expected the desire to taper off after their first encounter in the airport, but it hadn't. He'd wanted her again as soon as he'd had her, and nothing had changed since he'd had her again.

He wanted more. Didn't think he could get enough of her, no matter how many times he went back to the well to drink her in.

So, against his better judgement, he stood on her front porch, one hand curled around the color palette he'd borrowed from the hardware store, the other flexing open then closed in a nervous gesture he found impossible to control.

She'd seen through his charade this morning and played along. He supposed a single woman living alone didn't need everyone in town knowing she was sleeping with her house painter. He didn't have a clue how he would hide an affair from his brothers, particularly Rick, who he was working for and living with. In the past, the brothers hadn't had any secrets between them. If one scored, they all knew it. For reasons he didn't want to think about, he wanted to keep this to himself. Maybe it was because of the way his last relationship had imploded. He didn't trust his judgement, and his brothers would be quick to concur. He had no business starting anything with anyone at this point in his life. Distance provided clarity. The more time he put between him and what had happened with Jessica, the better his decision-making process would be.

Yet...he couldn't do it. He couldn't stay away from her.

Why the fuck did she have to end up in Willowbrook? Life would have been so much easier if he'd never seen her again.

He lifted his hand, knocked on the screened door. He was just about to knock again when the inner door swung open and every rational thought he'd ever had fled.

"You coming in?" She pushed the screened door open, inviting him in.

"Yeah, sure." He gave his head a little shake to clear it as he followed her inside. He'd never found sweatpants sexy, but on her—holy crap! He couldn't stop his gaze from raking over her from head to toe. *Shit*. He imagined taking her from behind, her damn hoodie thing wrapped around his hand. As his gaze traveled south, he licked his lips at the thought of pushing the T-shirt visible beneath the unzipped jacket up to her armpits, exposing the perfect breasts he remembered from the airport. He'd wanted to taste them then, but knew better. He'd been too close to the edge of his control. Anything more, and neither one of them would have made their next flight.

Pushing thoughts of her tits aside, he imagined how easy it would be to yank those elastic-waist pants down to her ankles—then off completely. He'd lay her back, spread her wide, and bury his face between her thighs.

"You brought the paint chips?"

The sound of her voice jolted him out of his daydream. "Yeah." He held the palette up, fanning it out. Did she really want to talk paint? He'd been pretty sure they'd been on the same page this morning. She could damn well go down to the hardware store and pick out her own paint colors. The palette had been an excuse for him to come back tonight for other things. The expression on her face told him he might have been mistaken.

"The light's better in the kitchen." She led the way, and he followed.

Was she expecting a repeat of last night? And here he'd been thinking about actually taking her to a real bed tonight. Something he hadn't considered before. It was darn near impossible to do it in bed without at least some face-to-face contact. Up until he'd unburdened himself to Jake, he'd been content with the less intimate position of taking her from behind. No eye contact involved. No kissing.

Now, he wanted more, and it appeared she'd changed her mind. Though he found the sweatpants sexy as hell, he doubted she did.

Fuck me. As she pulled two glasses from the cabinet and filled them with ice, he realized he wasn't going to get any tonight. Perhaps never again from this woman, and, presently, she was the only female his body wanted.

"Sweet tea or soda?" She pulled a pitcher of dark liquid from the refrigerator. "I won't vouch for this stuff. I'm just learning to make it."

What the hell? He'd welcome some hemlock right about now. Anything to put him out of his misery. "Sweet tea will be fine."

What am I doing? Kenzie poured two glasses of sweet tea, minus the sweet, and set them on the table. Tonight was about taking back control of this situation with Will Ingram. The arrogance she'd seen in his expression earlier had set her teeth on edge. It was one thing for him to know how much she wanted him and quite another for him to rub her face in it. She couldn't let him see how much she craved the raw sex she was afraid she'd only get with him. When he sank inside her, she forgot all about her practically empty bank account and her former boss/lover's betrayal. She almost forgot Will Ingram would never want to see her again once he found out who she was.

She should tell him, but she was such a chicken she might as well have sprouted feathers. The best she could do was put the brakes on their relationship, and the only way to do so was to make it clear she didn't want any more mind-blowing sex. What said "Not tonight, buster," better than a ratty old sweat suit she saved for rainy days when she had cramps? There was nothing like sitting around in cozy clothes, eating double-chocolate fudge ice cream, and watching sappy movies on cable to make a girl feel better.

However, she had the distinct impression she'd underestimated the man currently sitting across from her. Her trusty sweatpants and hoody might as well have been a sheer negligee for all the good they'd done her. She could still feel the heat of his gaze on her skin as he'd undressed her with his eyes. Oh, and the naughty things she imagined he would do to her once he'd gotten down to her bare skin. Will raised his glass to his lips. Kenzie did the same, downing a healthy swig of the brew she'd made three times as strong as recommended and deliberately left the simple syrup out of. It was all she could do not to gag on the bitter drink.

To his credit, Will smacked his lips and set the glass cautiously on the table. Then his gaze met hers and once again—they were playing his game, not hers. "What's going on?" he asked.

"I—"

"Are you trying to poison me? Because if you are, there are less obvious ways to do it."

"No. I. Oh hell. I don't know." She snatched both glasses and dumped the contents down the sink. Needing to keep her distance in order to think, she propped her hips against the cabinet and grabbed the countertop for support. "You said it last night. You don't want to want me. I feel the exact same way, and I don't know what to do about it."

Will raised one brow and slouched in his chair, his gaze more thoughtful than heated this time. "So, your solution is to fry my eyeballs with the ugliest garment you could find then poison me for good measure?"

"No. Well, yes. About the clothes," she hurried to add. "Not the poison. It's just very strong unsweetened tea. Harmless. Really."

"Let me explain a couple of things to you, Kenzie." Will stood then closed the distance between them. Kenzie sighed and her lids dropped as he placed his hands on her hips. "First, leave the making of sweet tea to the experts." His thumbs found the hem of her T-shirt, delving beneath it to stroke the skin at the edge of the waistband of her pants.

Kenzie fought for control. "And second?"

He dipped his head. His lips grazed her neck right below her ear then teased their way up to nibble at the lobe. Hot breath raised bumps on her flesh right before his voice sent a shiver down her spine. "These are the sexiest goddamn clothes I've ever seen, and I'm going to peel them off of you very, very slowly."

Kenzie groaned. She couldn't help it. She wasn't sure if his words were a threat or a promise, and she didn't care as long as he followed through.

"Should I take your groan as consent?"

He was big on consent, had asked every time they were together, and she appreciated his thoughtfulness even though every cell she possessed screamed for him to get on with it. Needing to feel his solid body, she let go of the countertop and gripped his shoulders. "How long is this going to take? I need to choose paint colors."

He nibbled his way across her jaw to the corner of her mouth. He raised his head then and, with one hand, tilted her face up to his. She hadn't been this close to his eyes since she'd sat down next to him in the airport bar. For a split second, she felt as if he could see her soul, every secret want and desire. Before she could decide what it was she saw in his, he broke the connection, his gaze going to her lips, parted in blatant invitation.

"You can choose paint colors in the morning." Then his lips were on hers in the hottest, wildest kiss she'd ever experienced. His lips were magic, taking, giving, coaxing hers to try and match what he was doing to her. When his tongue thrust past her teeth to stroke the roof of her mouth, her tongue entered into a duel, as eager to taste him as he was her. When he took her head in his hands, positioning her to his advantage, she gripped two fists full of his hair, joining the struggle for supremacy.

His lips abruptly left hers, but he didn't relinquish control of her head. His words were urgent, and she felt them rumble up from his chest now pressed hard against hers. "God, I love the way you take what you want."

Then he dove back in for more, and she did the same. She didn't know how long they stood there kissing each other like starved animals, and she didn't care. As far as foreplay went, it was the best she'd ever had, and they were still fully clothed. God help her when they got naked together. She'd probably die from the sheer pleasure of feeling his skin against hers.

He moved like lightning. Suddenly, her feet left the ground and her butt hit the counter. In a flash, she was naked from the waist up, her nipples hard. She didn't wait, couldn't. Hands cradling his head, she urged him forward as she arched her back. He took the hint. Taking both breasts in his hands, he palmed her left while he squeezed her right to the point of delicious pain. Then he took the distended point into his mouth.

"Oh, god!" Kenzie almost rocketed off the countertop as a bolt of white-hot heat shot from her nipple to her core. The tender tissues between her legs tingled then began to throb with an urgency she'd never experienced before. She worked her hips in an age-old rhythm meant to bring satisfaction, but only brought frustration at Will's slow pace.

Her nails dug into his scalp. "Please." *Please. Please. Please.*

The audible *pop* when he released her breast was as erotic as any sexy talk she'd ever heard. Cool air from the window air conditioner brushed the wet tip, making her shiver with need. Her mind scrambled to make sense of too many things happening at once—to grasp some scrap of sanity before she lost all touch with reality. Will squeezed her left breast hard enough to make her gasp. Then his mouth closed over the tip, and she was once again at his mercy.

Pleasure. God, what pleasure. And pain. And need. Desperate, aching need to see him, to touch him, to feel him moving inside her. It consumed her. Devastated her.

"Please." It was a weak plea from lips gone numb.

Another *pop!* and his face was in front of hers, his hands still doing wicked things to her breasts which made it difficult to think. "Please, what?"

"Please." It was the best she could manage, and inadequate in the purest sense of the word.

"Tell me what you want, Kenzie. Your pleasure is my pleasure."

God, he was too perfect for words. He couldn't be real. She skimmed her hands from the back of his head to his shoulders and down to his chest. "Strip."

His face turned to stone, every sharp plane and angle frozen. Had she asked for more than he was willing to give? The two times they'd been together before, he'd never fully removed any clothing.

Eyes burning into her, his lips barely moved. "God, I love a woman who knows what she wants."

He stepped back. In one smooth motion, he pulled his shirt over his head and tossed it aside. He threw his wallet on the counter beside her then shed his jeans and boxers at the same time as he toed off his shoes. No socks. God, so New York.

"What now?"

His voice jerked her attention from his strong, bare feet to his crotch where his cock stood erect and proud. Nothing to complain about there. Her gaze followed his treasure trail up and over his defined abs to his chest. Her nipples tingled as she imagined the way the light mat of hair there would feel against them.

He hadn't moved an inch during her perusal—a testament to his control. "I want to touch you."

CHAPTER TWELVE

Will clenched his jaw tight and took a step forward, putting himself within her reach. Giving her what she wanted.

Her fingertips brushed his bare shoulders. So soft, yet the bold way she explored his upper body set him on fire. He closed his eyes, hoping to retain control as long as possible as she learned every plane and valley of his torso. He had to be crazy. No sane man would endure this kind of torture.

After what Jessica had done to him, he'd vowed to avoid this level of intimacy at all costs, but he'd also vowed to avoid this woman. MacKenzie Carlysle was a force he couldn't resist. The way things were going, he might not ever have his entire life back, so why not take the parts of it he could? Beginning with this. And, lord, how he wanted this part of his life again.

His dick pulsed with need, his blood pumping through him like molten lava. As she explored south, he shifted incrementally closer, and bent to grip the countertop on either side of her hips. The move brought him close enough to nuzzle the spot on her neck where her pulse beat strong and rapid. She was as turned on as he was. Then she closed her fingers around his shaft. Control became a rope dangled just beyond his reach. He couldn't remain still when every fiber of his being screamed, *Fuck her!*

He acted on pure instinct. Flexing his hips, he thrust into the cradle of her palm then retreated and did it again.

Easy. Easy. Don't want it to be over before it even starts.

On the next withdrawal, she used her thumb to swipe a bead of pre-cum over the sensitive head. Will groaned and wrapped his left hand around her nape. He tilted her head to allow him maximum access then buried his face in the crook of her neck where he gave in to the primal urge to mark her as his. Clamping his mouth on her neck, he sucked her sweet-smelling flesh into his mouth.

Her left hand slid from his shoulder to the back of his head while the fingers of her right tightened around his erection. He wasn't sure who was in control, and he didn't care, as long as the pleasure continued. He'd had hand jobs before, but with her gripping him tight, he couldn't recall a single one. One thing was certain, none had felt this good.

Needing to put an end to this before it went too far, he peeled his hand off the countertop and wrapped it around hers, guiding her as he pumped into the circle of her fingers, slowly shortening his thrusts until he was barely moving. Only then did he lift his mouth from her neck to admire the red circle that would become his mark of possession within the hour.

A sense of pride filled his chest as he straightened and glanced between them. Their hands, entwined around his dick, had to be the most erotic thing he'd ever seen in his life.

"Fuck, woman. I've got to have you. Now."

"I need you, too." She tugged, urging him forward.

He could take her right there on the countertop. Fuck her senseless, but this time, he wanted more. He wanted to feel her beneath him. Wanted to take his time. Explore every curve of her delectable body. Bring her to the peak over and over until she begged him to let her come. "Grab my wallet." He dipped his head, directing her attention to the item he'd dropped on the countertop earlier. She picked it up then he dragged her to the edge of the countertop and off. She wrapped her arms around his shoulders and her legs around his waist. It was all he could do to keep from dropping to the floor and taking her right there, but, somehow, he managed to hold her tightly to his chest. "Bedroom?"

"First door."

He didn't need more direction. Her house was the mirror image of the one he'd grown up in. A few steps brought them to the door. Two more to the edge of the bed—a giant four-poster occupying most of the floor space. It could have been a futon and he wouldn't have cared. He dropped her. She bounced once then raised her arms above her head and lifted her hips.

It was all the invitation he needed. He hooked his thumbs in the waistband of her sweatpants and tugged them to her ankles then off. He looked at her bare pussy then at the clothes still in his hands. No panties. "Christ almighty," he growled. Tossing her pants aside, he spread her legs and went to his knees between them.

His heart skipped a beat as he realized what he was about to do. He'd wanted to taste her ever since he'd swept his fingers through her drenched folds at the airport. From then on, he'd wondered what she would taste like. She brought her heels up to the edge of the bed and dropped her knees, opening herself to him. Will placed his hands on the back of her thighs, pressed her knees up and wide open. Like a man lost in the desert for days without water, he dove headfirst into her wellspring.

At the first swipe of his tongue, she screamed and bucked her hips. Will wrapped his arms around her thighs, pinning her in place then he buried his face in her pussy.

She tasted even better than he'd imagined. Salty and sweet, and god, she was so fucking wet. He drank his fill then turned his attention to her pleasure. He explored her folds, taking time to fuck her with his tongue until she begged for his cock. Then he focused on her clit. A teasing nip here. A slow lick there. He smiled at the curse words flowing freely from her mouth as he took her to the peak then backed off, over and over again. When he couldn't stand another minute not being inside her, he fixed his lips on her clit and sucked gently. He felt the muscles in her thighs grow taut then he thrust two fingers into her channel, crooking the ends up until he found the tiny pad of flesh that would send her over the edge. Two light taps coupled with the gentle sucking on her clit was all it took. Her inner walls clenched around his fingers as he continued to work her clit with his tongue and lips. She rode his mouth like a rodeo queen determined to make the eight-second buzzer. He would never tire of hearing her shout his name in the same breath as the Almighty's. Every spasm was a trophy to be treasured forever.

As her orgasm waned, he gently withdrew to place a line of kisses on the inside of her thigh. She shivered and tried to clamp his head between her trembling legs, but he easily pushed them apart and rose up to cover her.

She felt better than good beneath him. Perfect. He wouldn't trade what he'd just done for anything, but nothing could compare with being inside her. Raising up on his elbows, he searched the bed for his wallet.

Kenzie felt as satisfied as she'd ever been, but she needed more. She needed to feel Will's cock inside her, stretching her. Filling her. It was as if there was a part of her missing, and somehow, only the man currently searching for a condom in his wallet could fill the emptiness inside her.

It was crazy. She barely knew him, and he didn't know her at all. But there was chemistry between them neither one of them could ignore.

She should tell him who she was, but as soon as he found out her role in the demise of his career, he'd hate her. Call her selfish, but she needed the human connection she found with him. When he filled her, she felt whole. When he moved inside her, she felt alive. When he made her body sing, she felt like a woman. And when he lost control, pulsing inside her, she felt invincible.

I can't give him up. Not yet.

Will settled on his knees between her legs. God, he was beautiful. Broad shoulders tapered to a narrow waist, and in between, every muscle group was present and accounted for beneath taut skin. A light pelt of dark hair covered his chest then narrowed, drawing her gaze down. Her pussy clenched with need at the sight of his imposing erection straining toward her. He'd found a condom somewhere and was in the process of rolling it on. Even his hands were beautiful. Artist's hands. She could imagine his long fingers holding a paintbrush, commanding the paint to bring his visions to life. Much the way he had brought her back to life in a dingy airport mini-hotel. "You have beautiful hands."

His eyes met hers. His lips lifted in a smirk. "That's what you see?" He fisted his sheathed erection, waving it to draw her attention.

"Your equipment is um...impressive." She licked her lips. "But your hands are...I don't know...sexy, I guess. I love to feel them on me."

"What else do you like?" He leaned forward, bracing himself above her on one arm while he guided his cock through her damp folds, notching it at her entrance.

"This." She lifted her hips in invitation as he teased her sensitive flesh. "God, you're big." She needed to feel him inside her. Stretching her. Filling her.

Braced above her on both arms, the tendons in his neck standing out with the strain of denying himself, he took her breath away. He flexed his hips, driving her farther up the bed with one smooth thrust. "You're so fucking tight."

Kenzie grabbed her thighs and pulled her legs up, spreading herself wide. "Fuck me, Will. Fuck me hard." *Fuck me hard enough to make me forget.*

Will groaned and, with an expression of utter concentration on his face, did as he'd been told. He pounded into her over and over again. The sound of flesh slapping against flesh filled the room along with the grunts and groans forced from their throats as his movement took them both to the highest peak and over.

Her orgasm began with a burst of something so sharp she wasn't sure if it was pain or pleasure. Then the blissful waves took over, coming one after the other as her inner muscles clenched and released around his invading member. Kenzie cried out and, letting her legs fall, gripped his locked arms like anchors while he continued to ride her.

"Fuck, you feel so good." Without breaking his rhythm, he managed to bring her legs up again, holding them over his shoulders. Seconds later, his thrusts became erratic then short and hard, as his orgasm tore through him. His roar rent the air. His cock pulsed as his hot seed flooded the end of the condom. He towered over her, a man destroyed by passion, devastated and beautiful at the same time.

With a long groan, he released her legs and collapsed on top of her, his face buried in the crook of her neck, his cock perfectly filling all her empty places. She wrapped her arms around him, holding him as she'd longed to do since the first time he'd walked away without a word. He wasn't walking away now. Their hearts beat the same wild rhythm against each other. Blunted pain, in no way associated with his weight pinning her to the mattress, radiated out from Kenzie's heart and infused every cell in her body.

Love.

How is it possible for something to feel so perfect and hurt so bad at the same time?

Long minutes later, Will withdrew and rolled off of her. While he disposed of the condom in the bathroom across the hall, she dove under the covers, hoping he would come back to her. As the minutes ticked by and he didn't return, she refused to let the tears stinging the backs of her eyes fall. At the sound of footsteps, booted ones, she sat up, clutching the covers to her chest like a shield. Will Ingram, fully dressed, leaned on the doorjamb, his legs and arms crossed. Faint light from the kitchen illuminated one side of his face, revealing his hardened features. Had it only been a few minutes ago since she'd witnessed pleasure written in every line of his face? Kenzie's heart hurt again—this time for a man who was so broken he refused to believe happiness could last longer than a few seconds.

"I've got to go. I'll be here in the morning to start work on the outside paint."

Kenzie nodded. "Okay."

She waited until she heard the front door close before she pulled the covers over her head and let the tears flow.

CHAPTER THIRTEEN

"Jake called looking for you."

Will toed his shoes off and kicked them beneath the table next to the front door. These old houses didn't have an entryway, much less a hall closet, and Rick had worked too hard restoring the old hardwood floors to have them scratched up by hitchhiking pebbles caught in the waffle-weave soles of his boots. "Did he say what he wanted?"

Rick's gaze remained on the show playing on the TV. "Nope. And I didn't ask. Figured if he wanted me to know, he'd leave a message."

Anyone who knew Rick couldn't miss the hurt contained in those few words. *Shit.* He hadn't wanted to add his problems to whatever else his little brother had going on in his head. Damn Jake for not making up a bullshit reason for wanting to talk to him. "Give me a minute to shower and we'll talk. Okay?"

"Whatever."

Will hated to leave Rick hanging, but he needed a clear head before he could talk about what had happened in New York, and he damn sure couldn't think straight with Kenzie's scent clinging to his skin. The woman got to him on a level he hadn't expected. He couldn't stay away from her and he'd made up his mind tonight not to even try. It was a battle he wasn't going to win. Hell, if he'd stayed in her bed another minute, he might have stayed all night, and waking up in the morning with a woman bordered on relationship status.

Still, as he stripped and stepped under the stream of hot water, his chest felt tight and he couldn't shake the feeling he'd screwed up. Again. Leaving her had been harder than it should have been. God, the sex tonight had been off-the-charts hot. When it came to passion, she was his equal in every way. He'd had rough, raw sex before, but with her it was...more. More intense. More intimate. He fucking couldn't get enough of her. When he was deep inside her, he wanted to be deeper. And he never wanted to leave. This evening, when he'd collapsed on top of her, he'd been amazed at how hard his dick remained as long as he stayed inside her, only going limp once he'd left her bed. The reprieve had lasted as long as it took to find his clothes and pull them on because the second he laid eyes on her again—laying naked beneath the covers of her bed—his dick jumped to attention. It took every bit of control he could muster to walk away from her. Even then, he'd walked around the block twice before he'd been decent enough to go home and face his brother.

Rick. *Shit.* Will regretfully washed Kenzie's scent off his skin then toweled dry and put on clean jeans and a T-shirt before heading down the hall. He stopped in the kitchen for a beer, needing something to do with his hands, and perhaps a little liquid courage. Telling Jake had been one thing. As a lawyer, he'd heard it all and didn't judge. Rick? Well, he wasn't a lawyer.

He grabbed his cell phone where he'd left it charging on the kitchen counter and pulled up the missed calls. As he strolled into the living room, he pressed callback for Jake's number. While it rang, he put it on speakerphone and tossed it on the coffee table. Rick muted the television and straightened in the new easy chair he'd bought to replace the old recliner they'd had as long as either of them could recall.

"You sure you want to do this?" Rick asked. "You don't have to."

Will sat on the sofa and kicked his heels up on the coffee table—another new purchase. "I don't want to, but I'm living with you. You have a right to know why."

"No, I don't." He made to stand just as Jake's voice came over the speaker.

"Will. Where the hell have you been?"

Will gestured for Rick to stay put. "I was out. What did you want?"

"Am I on speakerphone?"

"Yeah." Will ran the fingers of one hand through his hair. "Rick is here. He knows something is up. Might as well tell him."

"Your call, Will. It's always your call."

"I know. I'm tired of hiding my stupidity. Go ahead, tell me what's up."

"I'm going to put a private investigator on this up in New York. I read the file the NYPD sent, and there are several people on your list they didn't interview. Or if they did, the notes aren't in the file. Once he locates some of these people, I'll go up there and talk to them. I don't mind telling you, this whole thing stinks. They did a shoddy job of investigating. Plus, I want to talk to the officials at your bank. The signature on those withdrawals aren't anything like yours, yet they let Jessica withdraw a shit-ton of money without making any attempt to verify with the only signatory on the account. That's on them. Not you. At the very least, I should be able to get your funds replaced. But, it's the kind of strong negotiation best done in person."

"She fucking cleaned out your bank accounts?" Rick's heated question reminded Will of the boy his brother had been before he joined the Marines.

"They have her on security camera at three different branches the day before she disappeared." Will filled in the blanks for Rick. "She left me enough to cover my purchases for a few days. She was supposedly busy getting my gallery showing up and running, and I had my head buried in a canvas. Our paths didn't cross for those intervening days. I didn't know she was gone until I showed up at the gallery for the opening and found the place locked up tight. Not a painting in sight."

"Fuck. That. Bitch."

"What he said," Jake added.

"Apparently, she and the gallery owner, Cecil Hawthorne, targeted me from the get-go. It was an elaborate setup, months in the making.

The two of them disappeared off the radar with my savings and all my assets." Will paused to take a long draw from his beer. "I still don't understand why they took the paintings. They haven't shown up on the black market anywhere. I have enough friends in the art world, someone would have noticed and called me."

"It doesn't make sense to me, either," Jake said. "It almost seems like this is personal."

"How can it be? Jessica was my agent. She made money off every painting I sold." He stared at the bottle in his hands. "I was sleeping with the bitch, too. What else could she want from me?"

"Whoa!" Rick sat forward. "Wait a minute here. You were sleeping with her? For how long?"

"Since the night we met. A couple of years. Hell, she practically lived in my loft."

"Were you in love with her?"

He'd thought he was, but, as an image of MacKenzie Carlysle popped into his head, he knew his feelings for Jessica had never equaled what he felt for Kenzie and he'd only known her for a few weeks. "No. I don't guess I was. Hell, I never gave it any thought. We were fuck buddies."

"Did *she* know you were just fuck buddies?"

"What? Yeah. No." He ran his fingers through his hair again. "Fuck. I don't know."

"Hell hath no fury," Rick said.

"Like a woman scorned," Jake added. "This is starting to make sense now."

"Man, you are dumber than a box of rocks." Rick stood and sauntered into the kitchen.

Will spoke to the phone on the table. "You think she did this because I didn't...what? Propose?"

"Maybe," Jake said. "Women are inexplicable creatures. Let me ask you this. Do you think she loved you?"

Will let the question sink in as he drained the remainder of his beer. "I don't know. Maybe. We were a lot closer the first year or so we were together. I wasn't working as much. When she booked the gallery showing with Hawthorne for me, the pressure was on to produce enough paintings to fill the place. I was in the studio night and day for months. I guess we sort of drifted apart."

Rick sauntered back in with two fresh beers. He handed one to Will then resumed his seat. "Jake?"

"Yeah?"

"You have to find this bitch. She's holed up somewhere with Hawthorne. You find her, you'll find the paintings."

"Yeah, I suspect you're right."

"How much money did they take?" Rick asked.

Will named a figure. Rick whistled.

"That's a shit-ton of money, bro, but unless they're living on a shoestring, they'll blow through it sooner or later. Then what are they going to do? They'll have to come up for air."

"Hawthorne had money, too. Hell, they could be living it up on a beach in some third-world country for all we know."

Jake cleared his throat. "As far as I'm concerned, they can keep the money. The bank let the funds slip through their hands and they need to make it right. It's the paintings I want to recover. They're one of a kind—original W.H. Ingram's. I don't want them showing up when we're all dead and gone, selling for millions a piece at auction."

"I can paint more," Will lied. He hadn't picked up a paintbrush since the day he'd found out about Jessica's betrayal.

"You're missing the point, William."

Rick raised an eyebrow at their older brother's use of Will's given name. Will shook his head as he shared a silent laugh with his younger brother. Jake always did have a pompous way about him. "What is the point, Jacob?"

"I hear you snickering, Richard. Don't think I don't know when the two of you are laughing at me."

Will tried to wipe the smile off his face. "Go on, Jake. What were you saying?"

"I was saying, I'm going to get your fucking paintings for you then I'm going to kick your sorry ass if you so much as look at another woman for the rest of your life."

Another image of Kenzie popped into his mind. Will sobered immediately. Jake was right. He needed to stay the hell away from women.

They spoke for a few more minutes before Jake signed off. Will kicked back, relaxing now that the conversation was over and Rick knew everything. A few months ago, he couldn't contemplate telling his family what had happened. Since he'd spilled his guts to his brothers, he felt better about his future. If Jake wasn't able to recover the paintings or the money, he'd live. Maybe even paint again. Unbidden images of MacKenzie came to mind. He'd start with her eyes—

"So, you gonna tell him you're fucking BlackWing's new PR lady?"

Shit.

"Hell, no. And you aren't, either."

Rick shrugged. "Not my news to tell."

"Damn right it isn't." Will stood and stretched, the evening's activities suddenly taking their toll. "I'm turning in. Need to get an early start in the morning."

"Me, too. I put the ladders and the paint supplies in the truck earlier. We can drive down together if you want."

"Sure." They agreed on a time then Will shuffled off to his room, leaving Rick to finish the show he'd been watching.

As soon as the door closed behind him, Will went straight to the closet and dug out the box of art supplies he'd brought from New York. His hand trembled as he reached for the nearly empty sketchbook and his favorite set of pencils sitting on top of the expensive brushes and other items he hadn't been able to part with.

Sitting on the floor and using the bed as a backrest, pencil in hand, he stared at a blank page. His gut churned with anxiety. *You can do this. Just like his first drawing class at The Cooper Union. One line at a time. The first one's always the hardest.*

This was so much different than his first semester class though. Then, he'd doubted his abilities in relation to the other students, many of whom had come from fancy prep schools and charter schools devoted to the arts. He'd had a public school education in a small, rural Texas town where art classes were considered minor electives, not career preparation. He still considered it sheer luck he'd gotten in, and with a full scholarship to boot. Angels had been looking out for him then, and maybe they still were. Will placed the tip of the pencil on the paper and closing his eyes, sketched the first line, and the next, and the next. Only after he'd nearly completed the drawing did he open his eyes to see what he'd done. There, staring back at him was a reasonable likeness of the woman who captivated his every thought.

CHAPTER FOURTEEN

I'm so screwed. And she wasn't talking about what she'd done with Will Ingram the night before. The way they'd come together had been...special. More than just another good fuck. She'd bet her last dollar it had meant more to Will, too. She'd seen it in his eyes when he came, and felt it when his heart beat next to hers. He'd run this time, too, but he'd allowed her to hold him first. Those few minutes of silence had said more than any words could have. He cared for her. Probably not as much as she cared for him, but he did care.

Which was the reason she felt like shit.

I have to tell him.

This morning.

She put the finishing touches on her makeup then stood back to take a look. There wasn't enough concealer in the world to completely hide the dark circles under her bloodshot eyes. "That's what you get for crying half the night," she told her reflection. She applied her lipstick, a shade she hoped wouldn't clash with her eyes then once again examined the overall effect. *Not bad if you like zombies.*

"Promise me you'll tell him today."

Kenzie pressed her lips together, smoothing the glossy color. "I promise."

"And now I'm talking to myself. Great. Just great." With a sigh, she stepped into her heels and checked the buttons again on her blouse to make sure she'd fastened them right. Satisfied her second attempt had done the trick, she trudged to the kitchen to fill her travel mug. Tomorrow, she'd be getting her coffee at The Donut Hole since Rick Ingram was scheduled to begin demolition later today.

She filled her mug, washed the pot then moved the coffee maker to the kitchen table where Rick had said her few kitchen items would be fine for the time being. She'd just finished covering everything with the plastic sheeting he'd left for her when a loud clatter outside almost made her jump out of her shoes. Risking a peek through the window over the sink, she saw the source of the noise—a ladder had been placed against the side of the house. Will Ingram stepped into her line of sight. Her heart did a Vaudeville-worthy tap dance.

He'd been hot in his metro-sexual getup when she'd first seen him at JFK airport, but dressed in a paint-splattered T-shirt and jeans ready for the trash bin, he was hot with a capital H.

You promised to tell him, she reminded herself. *So, go do it. Now.* Kenzie wiped her sweaty palms on her skirt and forced her feet to move. Opening the back door, she stepped out onto the small concrete porch. "Hi."

Will paused two steps up the ladder. "Hi." His gaze raked over her business suit—one she'd paid too much for when she actually had money to spend on such things. It had been tailored specifically for her and fit like the proverbial glove. She'd chosen it this morning because she'd always felt more confident wearing it. Under his scrutiny, her body heated, and she felt her resolve to do the right thing evaporating. "You're...stunning."

"You, too." Kenzie ducked her head, hoping he didn't notice the flush she was sure had stained her cheeks bright red. "I mean...you look..." She waved up and down to indicate his person. "Good."

Christ. She sounded like an idiot. She wiped her palms on her skirt again then raised her chin, determined to get the words out before she did something really stupid like jump his bones. "Look, Will—"

"Hey, you forgot the paint scraper."

Kenzie jerked her gaze from the sexy man on the ladder as Rick came around the corner of the house, a tool in his outstretched hand. "Oh, hi, Ms. Carlysle."

She nodded and cleared her throat. "Mr. Ingram."

Will took the scraper from his brother then continued up the ladder. A second later, a screeching, scraping sound reminiscent of fingernails on a blackboard, sent a shiver up her spine. Flakes of white paint drifted down, creating a summer snowstorm. Kenzie stepped back to avoid having it land in her hair.

Rick joined her on the porch. "You heading out? I'm going to get the cabinets out this morning then. If I have time, I'll start to work on removing the old linoleum flooring."

"Oh. Okay." Rick followed her into the kitchen. Kenzie grabbed the mug of coffee she'd left on the counter. "I'll get out of your way, then."

"No problem. Figured we'd get an early start. Take your time."

"Not a problem. I was just leaving." Shit. She couldn't talk to Will with his brother around. She'd tell him tonight—if he came around. Would he? She had no idea, and she couldn't very well ask him. Theirs was a no-strings, no-obligations kind of relationship. Who was she kidding? They didn't have a relationship. They were fuck buddies—at best. There were no guarantees between them. No promises. No expectations.

"What time do you think you'll be finished today?" She slung the strap of her purse over her shoulder and snagged her keys off the hanger by the back door.

"I'll probably knock off around four o'clock. I suspect my brother will stop earlier. It gets awfully hot in the afternoon."

Kenzie nodded. "Okay. Call me if you need anything."

"Will do." Rick waved to her as she went out through the back door. She didn't look up at the man scraping old paint off her house as she made her way to her car parked in the driveway, but her awareness of him made her body hum and her heart ache. She couldn't imagine what his reaction would be when he found out who she was. One thing was certain, she'd never see him again. *How will I survive?*

She needn't have worried about Will's reaction because she didn't get a chance to tell him that night or the next or the next. After their first work day, he and Rick had arrived after she'd left and were both gone when she got home. They'd been there because the work was progressing and then there was the occasional note from Rick informing her where he'd moved something to, or asking her a question about her preferences.

At night, she ached for Will's touch, but he didn't come. So maybe the connection they'd made had all been in her head after all.

EVEN THOUGH WILL'S actions were hurting Kenzie, he couldn't help himself. He wanted to be with her every night. He wanted to tell her what she meant to him. But each night after he and Rick left her house, something else took hold of him and wouldn't let go.

So, he waited for his brother to go to bed then crept out to the garage where he'd cleared a space big enough for an easel and a stool. He'd found an old unused canvas in the closet of his room, a relic leftover from his high school art classes, and dusted it off. It was cheap, but he didn't care. It saved him from having to buy one. He didn't want people, meaning Rick and Jake, to assume he was painting again. He was dabbling. Trying to work a woman out of his system by putting her likeness on canvas.

It wasn't working.

If anything, he wanted her more than he had before. His fingers itched to feel her soft skin. His hands ached to trace her curves and his entire body ached to possess her. Staring at her likeness every evening until he forced himself to go to bed didn't help, either. She'd somehow gotten past the roadblocks he'd put up when his life had gone to shit.

From the moment he first saw her, he'd wanted her. A few months earlier, it wouldn't have surprised him. He'd always had a healthy libido. But Jessica's betrayal had affected him on a molecular level. He'd lost the need to paint. Food, sleep, exercise, hell, even the desire for sex of any kind had disappeared. He'd become a shell of a man—until he saw Kenzie.

The painting was stunning, if he did say so himself, but the familiar ritual of applying paint to canvas had done nothing to push MacKenzie Carlysle out of his head. Instead, he stood before the completed work and cursed himself for being a fool. He had no business getting involved with a woman at this point in his life. He had little to offer other than his body, and after the last time they'd been together, a purely physical relationship would never be enough. Not for her. Or for him.

He lifted his brush again to add a hint of rose to her skin tone then thought better of it and let his hand drop to his side. Stepping back from the easel, he studied his work. This one was done. Finished. Perfect.

Reclining on a bed, her auburn hair spread wantonly across a pillow, an expression part pain part pleasure on her face, she looked gorgeous and feminine and powerful in the throes of her orgasm. As he stared at it, he thought it might be the most honest thing he'd ever painted. The bold brushstrokes said this wasn't her story. It was her unseen lover's story. "*I* did this to her," it said. "*I* made her feel this way." Yet she held something back from her lover. He hadn't consciously put it there, but he could see it. Eyes clouded with pleasure hinted at a secret she held close. *What is she not telling her lover?*

God, he couldn't look at the painting and not want to fuck MacKenzie again and again. And he doubted there was a man on the planet who wouldn't feel the same way.

Sighing, he forced his gaze to the floor now covered with splatters of paint. He hadn't intended to paint Kenzie at such a vulnerable moment, but he'd had little say in the matter. In the past, he'd tried to explain his process to inquisitive gallery owners and reporters, and felt he'd only convinced them he was either a liar or outright crazy. Or maybe a little of both. The truth was, he didn't plan his paintings. They formed in his subconscious and somehow ended up on canvas. It was as if his hands were nothing more than tools his mind used to bring the images to life.

He painted because he was compelled to.

The compulsion had quieted for a few months, but it was back with a vengeance.

He tightened his fingers on the brush he still held and prayed the need would go away again. Life would be so much simpler if it did. He could go on painting houses. Maybe even get Rick to show him how to use a few power tools so he could help him with the inside work, too. Millions of people lived their lives in control of every little thing they did each day. They decided when to wake. When to sleep. When to eat. When to work. When to rest.

Not so with him. The need to paint ruled him. He woke, slept, ate, worked, and rested when the creative urge let him. And if it demanded only work? He worked.

When he'd lived alone, he'd learned to set alarms to remind him to stop and eat or sleep. Then he'd met Jessica, and she'd managed his life for him so he didn't have to remember to set alarms.

Maybe his art *was* a madness of sorts.

Van Gogh had been crazy. The guy chopped off his own ear, for crying out loud. Will didn't think of himself in terms of the old masters. He wasn't in their league, and he knew it. But he was good. Anyone with an eye for art could see it. He could paint landscapes as easily as he could do a portrait. It didn't matter to him. He painted what his subconscious wanted him to paint. And right now, it wanted more of *her*.

He glanced around the garage, looking for something suitable to use since he didn't have another canvas. Coming up empty, he rubbed the back of his neck and paced the confines of his tiny workspace. *Shit!*

There was no way around it. He was going to have to buy more canvases or take to painting murals on the garage walls. He wasn't against the idea. In fact, he wouldn't mind having a life-sized nude of Kenzie, but he doubted she'd think it was so great, and he sure as hell didn't want his brother seeing it.

His gaze landed on the completed painting again. Damn it all to hell. He couldn't—no, wouldn't—show it to anyone, much less sell it.

Fuck me. Leave it to his muse to get him started painting again but make sure he couldn't make a living off it at the same time.

Will dropped his brush in an open jar of turpentine then grabbed a smaller one from the assortment awaiting him in the same old soup can he'd used as a stand since he was a kid. Loading the brush with black paint, he carefully drew the stylized *W* he'd adopted for his signature on the bottom right corner of the painting then stopped. W. H. Ingram was dead. Blowing out a pent-up breath, he continued until the signature read, *William Ingram.*

Straightening, he added the smaller brush to the jar of cleaning fluid then stepped back. Deep inside, the pain of the last few months raged inside him still. Probably always would. But it defined another man, not the one who'd painted this woman whose pleasure made a man feel like a god.

The signature, much like the painting itself, symbolized a new beginning for the artist and for the man.

Maybe it was time to take another crack at living.

CHAPTER FIFTEEN

The bell on the door jingled as Jake Ingram entered the boutique gallery on the lower east side of Manhattan. Sunnyside Gallery, the sign outside said. The private investigator he'd hired had indicated the owner, one Sunny Sheldon, had been interviewed by the police and dismissed as irrelevant to the case.

He'd check her out first. Absolutely nothing was irrelevant until he said it was. Someone, or several someones, had screwed his brother over, and he wasn't going to quit until he found them.

"Just a minute," a feminine voice called out from somewhere in the back of the long, narrow shop. "Make yourself at home. I'll be right out."

Make myself at home. Hmph! Maybe it was because his brother was so damn good at what he did, or maybe it was because Jake didn't have an eye for art, but as he strolled around checking out the eclectic selection of paintings and sculptures occupying the small space, he came to the conclusion they were all crap. Maybe he was wasting his time coming here.

"Can I help you?"

Jake turned around, his elbow sending a bronze sculpture—subject unknown—teetering on its pedestal. The woman reached around him, grabbing the piece before it hit the floor.

"Good catch."

She held the item rather than put it back while he was still standing there, he guessed. "Not your style?"

Jake shook his head. "Nope. Not even sure what it's supposed to be."

She, however, was very much his style. Dressed in a suit obviously tailored to fit her trim, petite body, her yellow-blonde hair twisted into a fancy knot and secured with a tasteful gold hair ornament he'd glimpsed when she bent to catch the sculpture, she exuded class and confidence. Two things guaranteed to turn him on. Unless she'd discovered some miracle youth serum, she was close to his age. Maybe a bit younger.

"Not sure what your style is, or not sure what this is?" She held the item up so he could get a good look at it. He took the opportunity to check for a ring on her finger instead.

"Both, I guess."

She flipped the item over, examining it from all sides. "Hmm. I don't know what it is, either. Perhaps it was the artist's intention? Let each person see what they want to see?"

He didn't know about the artist's intentions, but he liked what *he* was seeing. Her. "Then I know it's not my style. I like my art straightforward. What you see is what you get."

"You're a realist, then."

He let his expression convey his lack of understanding.

"You like realistic paintings. Still lifes. Portraits. Landscapes. You like to look at a piece of art and know the artist intended to paint a bowl of apples or a tree-lined river bank. There's a photography exhibit going on right now at the Metropolitan Museum of Art you'd probably enjoy."

"I don't know. I might need someone to explain the photos to me. Interested?"

He almost forgot to breathe as she walked away from him, her pert ass swaying side to side in a dark-green pencil skirt he'd give anything to see her take off. She halted at an empty pedestal on the other side of the room. Setting the art object down, she spun on the toes of the sexiest shoes he'd ever seen on a woman. "Maybe. I don't go anywhere with strangers though."

Her comment jolted him back to the reason he was there in the first place. "Jake, ma'am. At your service."

"Sunny Sheldon. What brings you in today, Jake?" She swept her hand toward the relocated sculpture. "I know it isn't the interpretive art on display."

Sunny Sheldon lived up to her name. She dazzled from her blonde roots to her sparkling eyes to the tips of her shiny shoes. Sunny, indeed. She had a cheerful demeanor, but it was the sassy, sexy undertones of intellect making his dick stand up and take notice. Jake shook his head. "No, it's not. I'm looking for anything by W.H. Ingram."

She straightened her spine, her gaze taking him in from head to toe. "You aren't NYPD. FBI?"

"Why would you automatically think I'm law enforcement?"

"Because anyone who knows anything about the local art world is aware of what happened to W.H. Ingram's paintings. Is this some kind of sting operation?"

"No. I'm simply looking for my brother's paintings."

"Your brother?"

"William Ingram is my younger brother. I'm here on his behalf."

Anger poured off her in waves. "What makes you think I would know anything about the missing paintings?"

"Will said you sold a few of his a while back."

"Those were legal sales, and he was paid promptly, according to our standard contract. I'm sure I can locate the payment records, but I won't divulge the names of the customers who made those purchases. Shortly after I sold the ones he'd consigned with me, he acquired a new agent. I tried to get more of his work—they were very popular—but was turned down. I believe the words his agent used were, 'I've got bigger things in store for him.'"

Years as a trial lawyer had honed his ability to tell when a person was lying and when they weren't. In his opinion, Ms. Sheldon was telling the truth. "I'm sorry. I didn't mean to insult you. Will said you didn't have anything to do with the disappearance of his paintings."

His apology took most of the starch out of her, but he still had a ways to go before he was in her good graces again.

"I've never had anything but the utmost respect for your brother. He has an extraordinary talent."

"I agree." He hoped his smile was reassuring. "I'll be sure to pass on your regards to him."

"Oh. My. God. You know where he is! He's all right, isn't he? Please tell me he is."

"He's fine. He's moved back to Texas."

"Thank goodness. I've been so worried about him. I tried to contact him after things settled down, but no one seemed to know where he was."

"I'd like to ask you a few questions, if I may?"

"Sure. Sure." She fidgeted with the hem of her suit jacket, getting her emotions under control. He'd seen witnesses and clients do it before. He wondered why she was so emotional about his brother. Did she know more than she'd told the police? "Let me close up then if you don't mind, we can talk in my office? I'll fix us some tea."

He didn't want any damn tea. He wanted answers, and he wanted her. She turned the open sign around and threw the dead bolt on the front door. Jake followed her through a maze of angled walls and display pedestals, past an ornate desk with a computer terminal and a stack of business cards in a glass holder. "I only use this desk to finalize sales." She waved him on. "My real office is in the back."

She paused at a closed door. "Please. No comments about the clutter." He barely had time to process the comment when she opened the door and stepped inside.

The place looked like a tornado had hit it. Magazines were piled on every horizontal surface. She grabbed a stack off a leather armchair facing the desk and dropped them on top of another haphazard bunch sitting on the floor. Jake held his breath, waiting for the tower to topple, but after a few seconds of wobbling, it came to an unsteady stop.

"Have a seat." She indicated the now-empty chair as she slid between the end of her desk and a bookcase crowded with framed pictures and what he supposed were small pieces of art. But what did he know? He'd told her the truth. He liked the stuff Will painted and that was about it. The stuff on her shelves could have been priceless pieces and he wouldn't have had a clue. "I don't know about you, but I could use a cup of tea."

She shoved a mountain of books to one side of the credenza behind the desk to reveal an electric kettle. A couple of feminine-looking teacups, complete with matching saucers, sat nearby. He preferred coffee, but aware he'd already been rude to her, he answered in the affirmative. She set the pot then picked a couple of tea bags from a wooden chest she pulled from a shelf just above her head.

Fascinated, he watched as she prepared the very civilized drinks with a grace and economy of movement he couldn't ignore. He shifted in his seat to relieve the pressure building behind his fly. He forced his gaze away from her perfectly plump rear to the photos on the bookcase. Some were snapshots—the kind everybody had—of happy times. Her, he assumed, dressed head to toe in a puffy ski outfit, a ski lift clear in the background. Then there were the professional ones. One in particular piqued his interest. He rose to get a better look. "Is that you and Curtis Sheldon? The actor?"

She answered without turning. "On the red carpet? Yes. I think I was ten. Maybe twelve. It was the first time he took me as his plus-one to the Oscars."

"Wait. Curtis Sheldon is—"

"My father." She stood beside him holding a filled teacup out. "It's not a secret." He took the cup she offered. Relieved of the burden, she indicated several other photos he hadn't looked at yet. "I've been to nearly every one of his red carpet events since. Some of the photos turn out good, others not so much. These are my favorites."

Jake resumed his seat. "You're close to your father."

"I am. My parents divorced when I was young, but I've remained close to both of them." She sat behind her desk and stirred her tea with a dainty little spoon before taking a sip. "What about you? Your brother never talked about his family."

He wasn't there to talk about his family, but he reminded himself, he was on a mission. If telling her a few things would loosen her up a bit, he was game. "I'm the oldest of three boys. Then there's Will and the baby, Rick. Our mother passed when we were young, and none of us were close to our father."

"I'm sorry about your mother…and your father. You're lucky to have your brothers though. I'm an only child."

"Neither of your parents remarried?"

"Nope. They both claim the other was the love of their life. They just couldn't live together."

"Huh."

"Yeah. It's hard to comprehend, but if you saw them together, you would understand."

"You didn't go into show business?"

"No way." She gave a little shudder. "I was never any good at pretending. Both my parents could always tell when I was lying about something. What about you, Jake Ingram?"

"I'm a lawyer, just like my dad. Will and Rick escaped the family obligation gene."

"Speaking of William…is he painting? I'd heard rumors he'd given it up."

Jake shrugged. "I don't know. I don't think so. He will though. It's who he is."

"Please tell him I'd be happy to showcase anything he wants to send me. Given what's happened to him, I'd even pay him up front with a guarantee to split anything I make above my purchase price with him 50/50."

"You're sure you could sell his work?"

"Positive. You aren't the first person to ask about his paintings, and you won't be the last."

"Which brings me to the reason I'm here. Will wants his paintings back, and I aim to find them for him."

"What can I do to help?"

Jake pulled Will's handwritten list from his pocket and slid it across her desk. "Do you know any of these people?"

CHAPTER SIXTEEN

It had been nearly a week since she'd seen or heard from Will. After the night they'd shared the most incredible sex ever, he'd dropped off the planet. If she didn't know better, she'd think she'd dreamed him up—from the first moment she'd spied him in the airport, to the moment he'd held her and looked into her eyes as if they held the answer to every question he'd ever asked. But she hadn't imagined him. He was very real. And even if he never returned to her bed, he deserved to know the part she'd played in bringing down his career.

How he'd missed it, she didn't know. The attorney her father had hired for her had advised her to keep her mouth shut. She didn't actually have a hand in the crime committed against W.H. Ingram, but she'd worked for one of the people who had pulled off the crime of the century. No matter how she justified her innocence, it still came back to her being naïve. Stupid. Blinded by what she'd thought was love.

With her attorney at her side, she'd told the police everything she knew about her boyfriend/employer. In hindsight, it was pathetic how little she'd been able to tell them. Still, any relationship, good or bad, she might have with Will Ingram could only happen if she told him everything. Her father's lawyers could take their advice and shove it. She was done hiding things from Will. He deserved more from her. Unlike others, she hadn't set out to hurt him, but withholding her ties to the people who had undermined his career would hurt him. She could only hope, after the initial shock wore off, he'd come to see what they had together was strong enough to overcome the past.

She was still telling herself the fairy tale long after she'd deposited the take-out containers from dinner in the trash and snuggled in bed with a glass of wine and a romance book Melody had loaned her from her extensive collection. Three chapters in, she gave up hope Will would come over, and decided to wait for him to arrive for work in the morning. She'd tell him everything then. If it was the last time she saw him, so be it. At least she'd have cleared the air and maybe, just maybe, absolved herself of the guilt she felt for reducing one of the country's best artists to painting houses for a living.

After setting the book aside, she reached to turn off the bedside lamp when an insistent knock sounded at her front door. Startled, she glanced at the clock. Too late to be a neighbor wanting to chat. She grabbed her robe off the hook on the back of the bedroom door, jabbing her hands through the tangled arms as she hurried to the front of the house, her nose in the air, vigilant for any signs of fire. Why else would someone be banging on her door so late?

A quick glance through the peephole gave her the answer. Will Ingram stood on her porch, looking impatient and too sexy for words. Hand on the doorknob, her heart in her throat, she mentally ran through the short speech she'd practiced at least a million times over the last week. But as soon as she opened the door, he swung the screen door open and stepped into her space. He took her in his arms, pulling her tightly against him. His lips crashed down on hers, swallowing the words on the tip of her tongue and obliterating every thought from her head save one. Him.

She'd thought she'd known how much she missed him, but, surrounded by his strength, his scent filling her nostrils, his lips and tongue promising magic he could bring, she understood how desolate her life would be once he was gone. She craved his touch. Would never be the same without it. What could one more night in his arms matter? He'd still be gone in the morning, but she'd have one last memory of being his, if only for a short time, to sustain her through all the lonely days ahead. Because there would never be another man who made her feel the way he did. He was *the one*. The *only* one for her. But he could never be hers. Not when he learned who she was. What she'd done.

Kenzie melted against his hard body, gave herself over to the pleasure he alone could give her. He kicked the door shut behind him, and lips never leaving hers, walked her down the hall to her bedroom, undressing her with his hands as they went so when the back of her thighs met the mattress, she was completely naked, her heart in her eyes silently begging him to forgive her for not telling him before she'd fallen too far down the slippery slope of love.

I love him.

Had loved him since she'd first seen him in the airport in New York. Loved him before she knew who he was. Before she understood how completely he would own her.

Heart aching for the inevitable loss of something so special, she lay back on the bed and opened herself to him, inviting him to take what he wanted. Inviting him to give her what she needed more than she needed air to breathe.

As if he sensed her desire for actions, not words, with his hungry gaze raking over her, he stripped his clothes away. With equal hunger, she watched as he sheathed himself then climbed on the bed, his knees spreading her even wider. Then he was above her, the muscles in his arms and shoulders carrying the strain of his weight as he worked his hips until the head of his cock found her secret entrance.

His gaze locked with hers, dragging her into twin pools of swirling emotions. There was lust, for sure. And pain. Heartache so deep and dark she doubted a love, even as strong as hers, would be enough to repair the damage. He needed her. Needed to lose himself in her. Needed to feel the physical connection with another human being. Needed to feel alive. She knew the feeling too well. She'd needed him just as much back in Philly. Would always need him. Only him.

He flexed his hips, entering her, filling her, completing her with one powerful thrust. Hands on his biceps, she dug her fingers into his tight muscles and held on as he claimed her with a steady rhythm she matched, taking him as deep as possible on each stroke. She nearly wept as the now-familiar tightening began. God, it hurt so good. She never wanted it to end, but the pleasure on the other side of the pain beckoned to her, and too soon her body reached its limit. She threw her head back and dug her fingernails into his arms, dragging him down on top of her, an anchor as she crested the mountaintop and plummeted down the other side, clenching around his solid presence inside her, never wanting to let go.

Will's hands molded to her ass, tilting her hips to just the right angle, and sealing their bodies together from shoulder to groin. He rode her hard, prolonging her orgasm as he chased his own. He came with a roar of satisfaction she felt all the way to her toes. His cock pulsed inside her, his hot essence spilling into the condom. She'd never felt so much like a woman...or so broken.

This was what she would never have again if she told him the truth. Call her selfish, but as he lay atop her, still joined as intimately as two could be, his hot, ragged breath in the crook of her neck, she couldn't bring herself to tell him. Not tonight. Not tomorrow.

Someday in the future. Hopefully the very distant future when she was certain his love for her would overrule the pain her truth would bring him.

In the back of her mind, another truth she refused to acknowledge lingered. The future she envisioned might never come.

Their heartbeats slowly returned to normal, and though she welcomed his weight on her, he eventually rolled off her and padded across the hall to the bathroom. When he returned, she hoped he'd slide in the bed with her. Instead, he began to dress. Eyes closed against the pain of his leaving, she startled when something landed over her face. She swatted the clothes away—the ones she'd worn earlier and left on the floor in front of the closet.

"Get dressed."

"Why?"

"I want to show you something."

"What in the world? It's late." Kenzie tossed the bra he'd dumped on her head onto the floor. No way was she putting one of those on at this hour.

"I know, but this can't wait."

Curiosity got the better of her. Hurrying out of bed, she found a pair of sweat pants and a sweatshirt she liked to wear on a rare day off when she had nothing to do and pulled them on, forgoing her underwear altogether. Who would know? She stepped into a pair of canvas shoes, checked herself in the mirror over the dresser. Yep. She looked like she'd just been doing what she'd been doing. "Where are we going?"

"Don't worry. You're fine. No one is going to see you but me, and I like the way you look."

Knowing full well what he meant, she asked anyway. "How do I look?"

"Womanly."

Though she'd been teasing him, the way his heated gaze traveled over her and the gravity with which he'd delivered the single word made her heart skip a beat. A spark of warmth ignited deep in her womb and spread throughout her body. She felt powerful and more beautiful than she could ever recall feeling. Any thoughts she'd entertained about refusing to go with him evaporated like mist under the morning sun. "Oh."

He held his hand out, and when she took it, he tugged her forward until he could grip her waist. "Oh? That's all you've got to say?"

She nodded.

Then he fingered her waistband. Worked beneath it until his fingers brushed her trimmed curls. With a groan, she dropped her forehead to his shoulder and spread her legs, giving him access to her still-sensitive pussy. Two blunt fingers forced her open, making her knees weak and freezing her breath in her lungs. "You have no idea how beautiful you are when I'm inside you. Or when you come. Do you?"

She could barely think with him doing wicked things between her legs. If he didn't stop soon, she was going to come. "Please." *Please stop? Please let me come?*

He withdrew his fingers—cupped her swollen flesh in his palm and held her there—captive. His wanton sex slave. "Don't come yet. Not until I show you...."

"Show me what?"

"You'll see. Come with me?"

"Yes." Anywhere. If he planned to strip her naked in town square and fuck her senseless for all to see, she didn't have the will to refuse him.

He removed his hand from her sweatpants, patted her tender crotch then tugged her out of the house and down the street. Within minutes, he was unlocking the pedestrian door to his brother's garage. "Watch your step." He led her through the darkened space, eventually coming to a stop. "Stand right there. Don't move."

Will shifted to stand behind her, his talented hands on her hips, holding her flush against him. The unmistakable ridge of his arousal pressed into the small of her back, evidence of the power she held over him. "Close your eyes and don't open them until I tell you to."

"If you're going to show me a car or a truck, I'm going to kill you."

His laughter rumbled through his chest as he pulled her tighter against him. "Nothing so mundane, sweetheart." She felt his breath on her cheek. "Are you ready? Eyes closed?"

"Yes. Can we get on with this?"

He moved slightly, his arm still tight around her held her firm. Then there was a click and the room beyond her lids brightened. Anchoring her hips again, he leaned in and whispered in her ear. "You can look now."

Kenzie opened her eyes—blinked. Blinked again. Her mouth flew open, words trapped in her throat by her heart. A single lamp illuminated a canvas propped on a paint-spattered easel. It was the most erotic painting she'd ever seen—and it was her. Naked. Open. Vulnerable. One fisted hand on the pillow next to her head, the other clenched tight against her stomach just above her mons. Her nipples were hard buds, her breasts chafed from her lover's chest hair. And—most shocking of all—her facial features contorted, yet radiant. Kissed from within by passion and lust and...a love so pure no one could mistake her expression for anything else. This was what Will saw when she came for him. It took her breath away.

"What do you think?"

She worked her jaw, trying to force the words forming in her brain past her lips.

"This is how you look when you come." He fingered her waistband again. Then he touched her, begging for entrance. Without conscious thought, she opened for him.

Two fingers. Then three spread her wide. Worked in and out while his thumb caressed her clit. "Look at yourself. See what I see when you're beneath me." His fingers worked their magic on her. "Come for me, baby. Come, just like you are in the painting."

She shattered. Clamped her thighs as she rode his hand mercilessly, crying out his name between ragged breaths until her knees gave out and she slumped forward over the strong arm banding her waist.

Then she was on the tarp-covered floor. Will dragged her pants off—tossed them aside. Seconds later he was over her and in her. Fucking her. Hard. As merciless as she'd been moments ago. Staring up into his beautiful, shadowed face as he gazed up at her likeness—the one he'd painted from memory. She saw what she needed to see. *Love.* As tormented as her love was for him. He needed her as much as she needed him. She found the hem of his T-shirt. Ran her fingers beneath, over his taut skin until he shivered and cursed.

Power surged through her. She reached between them until her fingers found his shaft—felt his slick, engorged flesh filling her then retreating, over and over. When he hissed in a breath and drove into her harder, faster, she found her clit—worked it in tandem with his thrusts until she teetered on the edge of sanity. Only then did she throw her head back and gaze up at the painting.

Her inner muscles convulsed, gripping his girth, blinding her to everything but the feel of him inside her, the rightness of their joining, the beauty of being completed by the one man put on the planet for her.

As the muscle spasms eased, her vision returned, and, with it, the need to see him as he saw her. She framed his cheeks between her palms. "Look at me. Look at me when you come."

His gaze locked with hers. "Come for me, Will. Come for me."

His cock swelled, grew impossibly harder inside her. She saw the brief bite of pain cross his face, his clenched jaw, at the same moment he lost all rhythm and began to savage her with short, powerful strokes. His hot seed bathed her inner walls—all the while his gaze remained locked with hers.

If she could paint, she'd paint him just like this. Savage. Primal. Undone. But she was no painter, so she committed his beautiful, pained face to memory. An image to treasure at some unnamed point in the future when he would no longer be hers. When he'd find his muse in some other woman's bed.

KENZIE SAT IN ONE OF the old folding lawn chairs Will had found and set up facing the easel. He was painting again. Guilt was a living, breathing thing inside her. *I should have told him the moment I found out who he was.* It was too late now. He was painting again! He had a rare talent, and the world would be a better place if he continued to paint. She'd been part of the reason he'd stopped in the first place. If he knew.... "I don't know what to say."

"You don't have to say anything. I just wanted you to see it."

It was surreal to see a nude painting of herself—in a garage—in Texas. Even more surreal was the fact W.H. Ingram had painted it. "I thought you'd stopped painting."

"You mean, W.H. Ingram?" He didn't wait for her answer. "He did." He pointed to the lower right corner.

Kenzie leaned in to get a better glimpse at the artist's signature. "William Ingram," she muttered. Straightening, she locked her gaze with his. "Why?"

"I'm not the same person I was before. When it got down to it, I couldn't put my old name on it. Didn't seem right."

She'd seen portraits he'd done, but none of them conveyed the emotion this one did. It was stunning and maybe the most erotic painting she'd ever seen. "I can see why. I always knew you were good, but this is beyond good. It's—"

"Yours."

Kenzie gasped. "No! I mean, I can't let you give me the painting. Even with the new signature on it, you could sell it for a small fortune." She hated the thought of some anonymous person owning the painting, she couldn't deprive Will of the money he'd make if he sold it. He was too brilliant of an artist to be painting houses.

"I'm not interested in selling it, and I can't keep it here." He waved his hand around the darkened garage. "I'd put it in my room, but I'd never get any sleep looking at it."

Imagining why he wouldn't get any sleep with this painting in his room had Kenzie placing cool fingers on her heated cheeks. "Still, I don't feel right about taking it. Besides, where would I put it?"

Will continued as if he hadn't heard a thing she'd said. "I think I captured your expression well."

God, it was a good thing the only light in the detached garage was the one trained on the painting. Kenzie felt her cheeks glowing. "I wouldn't know."

"You know I got it right. What I want to know, what everyone who sees this will ask, is, what is she thinking?"

They'll think I'm a low-down, lying, weasel. She closed her eyes and pressed her lips together to keep the truth from spewing out. He didn't deserve what had happened to him, and she didn't deserve to be his muse. She was going to burn in Hell for what she was about to do, but she couldn't tell him—couldn't hurt him anymore than she had already.

Kenzie took in a deep breath, let it out. While focused on the painting, she took his hand in hers and laced their fingers together, and told him the other truth he probably wasn't ready to hear. "She's thinking how much she loves the man who put that expression on her face."

CHAPTER SEVENTEEN

Will stood and threw a tarp over the painting then, hands fisted on his hips, he stared at the cobweb-covered ceiling and tried to process what Kenzie had just said. She couldn't love him. It was the sex talking. All those orgasms, like the one he'd captured on the shrouded canvas, had muddled her mind. His fault. He'd take 100 percent of the blame. He should have stayed away from her. Should have painted a fucking landscape when the urge to paint had come upon him.

Yet, he couldn't deny he felt something for her, too. Was it love? Hell, no. But it was more than lust and more than like. How could he not feel something? She'd given him things he'd thought lost forever—physical desire and perhaps, the desire to live since painting was his life.

He owed her, but he wouldn't lie to her.

Shuffling behind him alerted him moments before she came to stand beside him.

"Too soon, I know." Her voice cracked a little, making him feel like a total ass. He did manage not to flinch when she lightly touched his arm. "I'll be going now." He took her hand, intending to offer to walk her home, but she shook her head and withdrew from him. "I'm a big girl. I can walk a few blocks by myself."

He couldn't find a single word to say, so he nodded. She held her ground as he leaned down to place a platonic kiss on her cheek. Hearing the door close behind her, he sat and stared straight ahead, silently cursing himself for being such an idiot. He'd let love blind him before. He wouldn't do it again. He'd thought Kenzie was in it for the sex, just as he was. Women were inexplicable creatures, and his track record confirmed he knew nothing about them.

He'd never intended to hurt her. Use her, yes, but she'd known the score. Hell, he never would have approached her in the Philadelphia airport—not in the state his mind had been in at the time. She'd initiated their first encounter, and he'd used her boldness to justify the way he'd taken what she'd offered and left without a word. Shitty behavior, but she'd had no right to expect more.

By some stroke of Fate or maybe karma had a hand in it, they ended up in the same small town where it was virtually impossible to not run into each other. He'd given her no reason to think anything had changed between them. They were two adults engaging in adult activities for the sheer pleasure of it. Nothing more. Until the other night.

He'd had an insane desire to see her face when she came. It wasn't supposed to mean anything, but it had. From the moment she'd touched him, he'd been lost to the swirl of pleasure he'd thought his ex-girlfriend's betrayal had taken from him forever. The fire in his blood had felt so damned good, and to see his desire mirrored in her gaze had broken through the wall of ice around his heart. He'd taken everything she offered, and he'd given a part of himself in return.

In the end, she'd given him more than he'd given her. The painting hidden behind his brother's discarded tarp was proof. He was painting again. W.H. Ingram no longer existed, but in his place, someone else had arisen. William Ingram. W.H. had a narrow vision of the world, influenced by what could be seen by the naked eye. William didn't live within those constraints. He exposed the hidden emotion, the secrets behind the surface beauty.

He'd been shocked by Kenzie's response to his question. Closing his eyes, he brought the painting to mind. She'd been correct, but love wasn't the only thing he'd brought to light through her expression. Had she seen the guarded secret and chosen to keep it to herself—as all good secrets were. Or had she simply not seen it?

The mystery was more obvious to him than the love and was why he'd asked the question, "What is she thinking?"

What are you hiding, MacKenzie Carlysle?

"Hey, Will!"

The sound of his brother's voice startled Will awake. It took all of a second to realize he'd fallen asleep sitting upright in an ancient lawn chair. In the garage! *Shit!* Heart pounding, his gaze flew to the painting. Thank God he'd left it covered.

"What the hell are you doing out here?"

Will stood, stretching muscles he wasn't sure would ever be the same. "I couldn't sleep."

Rick flipped on the overhead lights. Will's eyes protested the glare, but the sound of his brother's approaching footsteps cleared his vision like nothing else could.

"You're painting again."

The evidence, brushes, paints, and a recently used palette scattered on his dad's old work table, not to mention the tarp-covered easel, made it impossible for him to deny his brother's observation. "Maybe. Thought I'd give it a try."

"That's fantastic, bro!" Rick pointed to the giant white elephant in the room. "Can I see?"

Will shook his head. No fucking way was he going to let anyone see this painting other than the subject. It was too personal. And, he'd painted it without her knowledge or consent. In his mind, the portrait belonged to her. "Not this one. Maybe the next one. I'm still feeling my way around the painter I am now."

Rick stuck his hands in the front pockets of his work jeans and nodded. "Okay. I don't have a clue what you mean, but I can wait. I'm just glad you're painting again."

Will forced a smile. "Don't worry. You haven't lost your house painter. I'm getting used to the physical work. It's good for me, I think."

"Not if you stay up all night creating masterpieces. You can't do both, Will."

"I know. I need to find a balance." He turned away from the canvas. "And I will. I promise. I won't let you down."

"Well, if you need to take today off, go ahead. You're almost done on the outside of Ms. Carlysle's house, and I don't want you falling off a ladder or something."

The brothers walked toward the pedestrian door single file. Will flicked off the lights and locked the door behind them. "No worries. I could use some coffee and a shower though."

Rick jiggled his truck keys in his hand. "Take your time." He took a step toward his pickup then turned around. "Oh, and give Jake a call? He's been looking for you."

"Left my phone in my room." He shrugged. "No distractions."

With a slight lift of his chin to acknowledge the excuse, his brother resumed his course. "I get it." He climbed into the cab and leaned out the window. "See you in a few."

Will gave him a thumbs-up then climbed the stairs to the porch. He fixed himself a cup of coffee then made a beeline to the shower. Whatever Jake wanted could wait until he'd cleared his head. Unburdening himself to his brother had helped him get on the road to a new normal, but, as good a lawyer as Jake was, Will doubted he'd be able to recover any of the material things he'd lost. For months, he'd deluded himself thinking having the money back, or the paintings, or both, would solve his problems. The painting hidden in the garage was proof none of those things mattered. Losing them had broken him in some fundamental way, but being with Kenzie had put the shattered pieces together again, albeit in a totally different configuration.

As he soaped and rinsed, he tried to see the bad side in the changes he saw within himself and came up empty. He'd lost a small fortune, but he'd gained new insight. And it showed in his new painting. Artists were known to go through phases as they experimented and grew with their craft. Look at Picasso. He'd gone through over half-a-dozen phases in a span of less than thirty years. He wasn't a Picasso or anything close, but like the famous artist, his life had changed, and with it, his art.

He'd be fooling himself if he thought being with Kenzie had nothing to do with the change in him. She had everything to do with it. What it meant, he didn't know and wasn't in any hurry to figure out.

His phone rang again as he pulled the front door closed behind him. Jake. The man had something to say and, as usual, he wasn't going to give up until Will answered. Tenacity was probably a good trait for a lawyer to possess, but it was damn irritating in an older brother. Will leaned against the porch railing. "I'm here. What do you want?"

"Where the fuck have you been? I've called at least a dozen times and left messages. I even called Rick to make sure you were still alive."

"I left my phone in my room overnight."

"I ask again, where the fuck were you if you weren't in your room all night?"

"I was in the garage."

"Doing what? Or do I even want to know?"

"It's none of your business."

"You always were the weird one."

Having acquired what little sleep he'd had in a busted lawn chair, Will was tired and short on patience. "What do you want? I'm late for work."

"I've got good news and maybe not-so good news. Which do you want first?"

"Give me the good news first." He'd had so little of it lately, he craved it.

"Good news is, the bank has agreed to restore your funds."

Will grabbed the railing with his free hand to steady himself. "What? How the fuck did you manage that?"

"I had a little talk with the president. Explained to him how one of his tellers had let an unauthorized person have access to your accounts without even so much as a phone call to verify it with you, and how the teller's actions could result in legal action against the bank if the funds weren't replaced immediately. It didn't take long for him to investigate and come up with the truth. Jessica signed her own name to the withdrawal slips and yours was the only authorized signature on both accounts. They were liable, and he knew it."

"Christ, Jake." Will took a deep breath and let it out. "Does this mean I'm not a pauper anymore?"

"Depends on how much you had in the accounts but I'd say you're flush."

He'd had too much in both his checking and savings accounts. He should have moved some of it or invested it or something, but finances weren't his thing. As long as he could pay his bills and eat, he was good. Maybe it was time to hire someone who knew their way around a financial portfolio. "Thanks, Jake. I mean it man. I owe you."

"You don't owe me anything. You're my brother."

"Still. I owe you. I swear I told the bank manager the same thing and got nowhere. I don't know how you did it, but I'm grateful."

A loud sigh came across the line. "Hold onto your gratitude until you hear my other news."

"Seriously? You could tell me Jessica burned all my paintings right now and it wouldn't phase me."

"No sign of the paintings yet, burned or otherwise. However, you know the new PR person Hank hired? MacKenzie Carlysle?"

Every muscle in Will's body tensed. He gripped the top rail until his fingers screamed. He forced his jaw to unclench. "Yeah. What about her?"

"She wasn't on the list of people you knew in New York."

"Because I didn't know her in New York. I met her in the airport in Philly when our plane made an emergency landing."

"The police interviewed her. In fact, she was one of the first people on the scene the night of your gallery opening."

"I don't understand. Who is she?"

"She was Cecil Hawthorne's girlfriend and did PR for his gallery."

Will's legs gave out. He sank to the porch and cradled his forehead in his free hand. His gaze landed on the garage where the first thing he'd painted in nearly a year rested beneath a filthy tarp. MacKenzie Carlysle. Nude. With love and secrets in her eyes. Secrets no longer hidden.

Fuck it all.

Fuck her.

Shit.

This couldn't be happening. What kind of game was she playing?

"Apparently, she arrived at the gallery early to supervise the caterers and found the place locked up and empty. Instead of calling 9-1-1, she went home and tried to locate her boyfriend. According to the police report, when he was still missing the next morning, she went to the station to file a report. I don't know who put the missing person case together with the heist of your paintings, but someone did. They interviewed her and quickly came to the conclusion she didn't know anything. I don't have any way of determining if they were right or wrong, but I thought you should know."

"Thanks, man." What else could he say? His brother was doing him a solid no matter how devastating the news was. "How did you find all this out?"

"Remember the gallery owner you had on your list, Sunny Sheldon?"

"Yeah. Nice lady. She sold several paintings for me and was always trying to get more." He massaged his temple where a massive headache was forming. "Should have let her have them all." Hindsight was 20/20.

"It might have been a wise thing to do, but too late now. Anyway, I asked her to check a list of names and see if she recognized any of them. She knew several and vouched for all of them. Seems the Carlysle woman did some work for her when she first moved to New York. They kept in touch. When Hawthorne was a no-show after a couple of weeks, she approached Ms. Sheldon, looking for work. Sunny didn't need her services, but here's the interesting part—some of those paintings Sunny sold for you?"

"Yeah, what about them?"

"She sold them to Melody Ravenswood."

"Hank's wife?"

"She wasn't his wife then, but she bought one of the paintings for him and a couple of others for gifts to family members. Anyway, the two of them became friends and still are. Every time RavensBlood comes to New York, they all get together. Hank mentioned he needed a new PR person the last time he was here."

"She hooked them up?"

"Yep. So, as much as I distrust coincidences, I have to concede this is a genuine one."

"No chance Sunny Sheldon was involved in this somehow?"

"Not a chance."

"How can you be so sure?"

"Trust me, Will. She didn't have anything to do with your paintings going missing."

Sunny Sheldon had been one of the first people to take a chance on him when he first started out. When he was in college, she sold a few of his early works for enough to keep him from having to wait tables in order to eat. He'd repaid her kindness by giving her a more than generous commission on several of his later works. He didn't want to believe she'd be a part of what had happened to him, but what did he know? He'd trusted Jessica and look where his naivete had gotten him. Still, Jake sounded certain. The ability to ferret out liars made for a good attorney. Jake was as good as they came. If he said Sunny didn't have anything to do with the crime, then Will believed him. "I believe you." Then it hit him. "Where the hell are you? New York?"

"Where else would I be, asshat? I did all I could do over the phone. It was time to meet face-to-face with some of these people. I'm glad I did. You're getting your funds back, and I hope to at least pick up a scent regarding your stolen paintings."

"I hear a but in there."

Jake's laughter helped lighten Will's mood. Dredging all this up again was twisting him up in knots. "But," he dragged the word out. "I need you to help me out."

"I'm not going back to New York. You're on your own, big brother."

"No. Don't need you here. I need you to ask MacKenzie Carlysle a couple of questions."

Well, shit. "I'd rather go to New York."

Silence stretched over the miles until it became uncomfortable. Then Jake spoke. "Jesus, Will. Tell me you aren't fucking her?"

"It's none of your business, Jake. Just tell me what you want me to ask her."

"This isn't good, little brother."

"I won't disagree with you, but it's nothing. Just hooking up." His stomach revolted at the lie. "What do you need from her?"

"You know we talked about the trip you and Jessica made upstate?"

"Yeah, what about it?"

"Ask Ms. Carlysle if she ever heard Hawthorne talk about any place upstate. Did he take any trips out of town? If so, does she have a clue where he went? She might have seen something or read something in his office or an email. Anything along those lines. Think you can handle that?"

The dull thud in his temple now felt like a rock band was practicing inside his skull. "Yeah, I can handle it. When do you need to know?"

"ASAP, dickhead. I'm in New York. This is costing me a fortune. The sooner I get home, the better."

"Okay, okay. I'll borrow Rick's truck and drive out to Hank's place in a few. Catch her at work."

"Don't accuse her of anything, Will. We have absolutely no proof she's done anything wrong. The police believed her, and Sunny vouched for her, too. She's most likely a victim of all this, same as you."

He wasn't convinced. Not by a long shot. "I'll call you later." He ended the call and dropped both his hands to the porch floor. What a clusterfuck.

CHAPTER EIGHTEEN

Will sat on the porch until his ass hurt as much as his head, before going inside to take a couple of over-the-counter painkillers. After splashing his face with cold water, he resumed his walk down the street to where his brother was working.

"I've got to run an errand for Jake. Can I borrow your truck?"

Rick tossed him the keys. "When will you be back?"

"Don't know. Couple of hours?"

"Let me get my shit out of there, then." They walked outside together, and Will waited while his brother gathered up the tools he'd need for the rest of the day. "I'm good." Rick hefted an overflowing toolbox out of the bed of the truck and slammed the tailgate.

Will nodded. "Thanks. I'll finish the outside painting tomorrow." Then Rick would expect him to start on the inside walls. *Shit.*

"No worries. I've got a couple more weeks of work. It won't take as long to paint the rooms she wants done."

He put the truck in reverse. "See you later."

The drive out to the house Hank had inherited from his maternal grandparents took forever. As he followed the familiar road, he couldn't help but remember the times he'd run wild there along with Hank, Randy, and Chris. Life had been simple then. Go to school. Eat. Sleep. Play as hard as you could. It had all gotten complicated somewhere around the time he hit puberty and began to notice girls. Here he was, pushing the thirty year mark and women were still complicating his life.

His fault. He had a knack for choosing the most deceitful females on the planet. Which brought his thoughts around to the reason he was driving this nostalgic road in the first place. MacKenzie Carlysle.

Was she playing him? Again? Had they ended up on the same flight by coincidence? Or could it all be some elaborate scheme to...what? Finish him off? Make sure he never painted again? He didn't want to believe Sunny Sheldon had anything to do with stealing his paintings, but the link between her and MacKenzie and Cecil was awfully convenient. Still, coincidences did happen, and just because you knew someone who turned out to be a scumbag didn't make you one. If it did, he was guilty by association, too. He'd known Cecil and Jessica, two of the biggest scumbags on earth.

He couldn't dismiss the fact Kenzie had lied to him. When he'd followed her out of the diner and accused her of being a reporter, she'd claimed to have just discovered his identity and had been quick to tell him she wasn't looking for a story. If she'd mentioned her former association with Cecil Hawthorne then, he wouldn't have touched her. Ever. Hell, he probably would have borrowed money from Jake and got the hell out of town. Left her there to her new life and moved on. Starting over someplace else wouldn't have been easy, but it would have been preferable to getting caught up in her web of lies.

The road curved, and the big white barn with the black wings painted on the side came into view. Too bad all the good memories he had of the place, before and after Hank had converted the old barn into headquarters for BlackWing, would be tainted by seeing her there.

Hank had made a few improvements since the last time Will visited. What was once a gravel parking lot dotted with weeds was now a sleek blacktopped area, complete with striped slots wrapping around the back of the barn, out of sight from the house. The first few were marked for visitors. Will chose one, swung the old truck in, and cut the engine. Heart pounding, he stepped out. As he approached the new pedestrian door Hank had added to this side of the barn, he paused to take in his surroundings. The house and barn were a nod to civilization in an otherwise pristine landscape he'd always loved. Cotton fields stretched out in every direction as far as he could see. Off to his left, if he walked long enough, he'd run into a branch of the small river Willowbrook had been named for. God, how many hours had he and his friends spent there fishing, swimming, just laying around in the shade of a tree, talking about nothing and everything? Will smiled at the memory. Many of his early paintings had been of that very spot. Had he ever told Hank? He couldn't remember. He should someday. Hell, he should have sent one to his friend as a thank-you for the inspiration the trips out to this farm had provided.

Will glanced up at the restored barn, now offices and a recording studio for a world renown rock band. Who would have thought it? Hank had done well for himself but had stayed true to who he was—a small town guy who loved the land and honored the past. Will wished he could say the same for himself. He'd gone to New York, determined to let the grit of the city scrape away his small-town veneer. It had done a good job, scraping him down to the bone and spitting him out. Here he was, in Willowbrook, wearing skin he didn't recognize.

The city had fundamentally changed him, made him a great painter in some ways, an idiot in others. It had given him a life, an identity, and it had taken it away as soon as he let his guard down.

No more. He was home and he planned to stay here. The woman he'd come to see could get the hell out of his town. Move the fuck back to New York. Find some other sucker to play, to grind into the pavement.

But first, he wanted answers. What did she know? How involved had she been in Hawthorne's business? Where the fuck were his paintings? Most of all, he wanted to know, why him? What had he done to deserve what they'd done to him, to his career?

Then, muse be damned, he never wanted to see her again. If it meant he'd never paint again, so be it. He'd deal. He was starting to like house painting. It was good, honest work and kept him in shape. Hell, maybe he'd go into the remodel business with Rick. It wasn't the worst idea he'd ever had.

Forcing his feet forward, he stepped inside. Having never entered through the new door, it took a second to get his bearings. The sound of high-pitched squeals and disjointed banging drew him down the long center hall to an open office door. Hank's office. Standing in the doorway, Will took in the scene. What had once been an office fit for a rock and roll king looked like a cross between an executive office and a daycare center. His friend's beloved Ludwig drum kit still occupied most of the back wall, with a desk and electronic keyboard off to one side. Will noted the fancy computer monitors and what appeared to be about a million bucks worth of high-tech gizmos on top of the desk. Childhood artwork was haphazardly taped to the free spaces between framed platinum and gold albums and pictures of Hank with celebrities and dignitaries from around the globe. A pink toy stroller, complete with baby doll, sat to one side of Hank's desk. Smack in the center of the room sat a tiny drum set. A pixie with wild curls and bright-blue eyes held court behind the miniature kit, banging away with gleeful abandon while her foot-tapping dad indulgently looked on from a giant beanbag chair taking up most of the remaining free space in the room.

Will crossed his arms and leaned against the doorjamb to watch the concert. The more he listened, the clearer everything became. What at first had sounded like noise was indeed a simplified version of one of BlackWing's most famous songs. Damn if the kid wasn't half bad, at what, three years old? A perfectionist, too, like her dad, he determined when the child missed a beat, and a pout marred her adorably cute face as she paused then tried the bridge to the chorus again. Nailing it the second time around.

"Perfect, Gloria. You've got it, girl!"

The pride and love in Hank's voice twisted something deep in Will's gut. He'd never given much thought to having kids, but seeing this pint-sized version of Hank brought a lump of longing to his throat. What would it be like to find the right woman and have a couple of rug rats? Maybe one would inherit his talent with a paintbrush. Or not. He wasn't sure passing the creative gene on was such a good idea. It was hard as hell to make a living putting paint on canvas. Practically impossible, yet he'd done it for a number of years. Still, he wasn't sure he would wish the creative angst onto anyone, especially his own son or daughter. He'd do nearly anything to spare his child from the pain of ripping emotions from their chest in order to put them on display for the world to see.

He'd done it countless times, though if he was honest, not so much toward the end of his career. He'd still been driven by the need to paint, but there at the last, he'd done so with a voice in his head telling him to paint what people wanted to buy instead of what his gut told him to paint. It was Jessica who had convinced him to do the more commercially viable paintings. He'd argued, but eventually given in and painted what she wanted. She'd been right. They sold well and for prices he still couldn't fathom. He told himself he was happy, practically mass producing art for living room walls. The truth was, he'd been in a rut of his own making. It had taken another woman to shake him out of it.

Closing his eyes, he brought to mind the painting in his brother's garage. Just thinking about it made his heart rate accelerate and his fingers itch to grab a brush. To try again. To dig deeper. To expose her every emotion. Her every secret. Every lie she'd ever told. To put it all on canvas in paint tinted with his sweat. His tears. His blood.

No matter what she'd done to him in New York, she'd cut him to the core in Willowbrook. There wasn't a drop of blood on the painting, nevertheless, he'd bled over it. He'd turned himself inside out to expose what he'd seen in her eyes, and, knowing her secrets, he hated her. He hated who she was, what she'd done. Hated every breath she took.

Yet...he loved her with a fierce pain no amount of paint on canvas could cure.

He was so fucking screwed.

CHAPTER NINETEEN

The solo concert came to an end, shocking Will back to the here and now. As his friend sprang from his front row seat to envelope his daughter in a bear hug and pepper her with praise, Will began to clap. Startled eyes turned his way and, when recognition dawned, became soft and welcoming.

"Damn. Will Ingram." Hank scooped his daughter up, resting her on his left hip as he waved Will into his office. "It's good to see you, man." They shook hands. "Gloria, baby, this is one of my oldest and best friends. He paints pretty pictures."

Up close, he could see the child's resemblance to her mother was dominant, but her eyes were all Hank.

"Will, this is Gloria."

Will brought her tiny hand to his lips and placed a smacking kiss on her knuckles. She jerked her fingers out of his grasp, tucking them in close while she made up her mind about him. "Pleased to meet you." He nodded at her drum kit. "You put on quite the concert. Are you getting ready to go on the road?"

Hank laughed. "Don't give her ideas, buddy." He hugged his daughter tight. "She's got more talent in her little finger than I have in my entire body. If she wants to, she'll take the music world by storm one of these days."

Did he detect a bit of wariness in Hank's declaration? "Do you want her to go into the family business?"

"Heck, no! But Mel insists we let her explore her interests and talents. Not surprising, given the way she was raised."

"Oh?"

"Yeah. Long story best told by Mel herself. Come for dinner sometime and she'll fill you in." Hank addressed his daughter. "What do you say, Glo? Want Will to have dinner with us sometime?" Shaking her head, the child tucked her face against her father's shoulder, giving Will the side eye.

"Hey, pumpkin." He jostled her. "Better get all the facts before you make a decision." He pointed to the wall behind Will. Will turned. Christ. It was one of the paintings he'd consigned with Sunny Sheldon. It depicted a man and woman walking along a worn trail toward a copse of trees. A black dog ambled along behind them. It was Willowbrook, and the couple could easily pass for Hank and Melody Travis. "That's one of your favorite pictures in the whole world, isn't it?" Dark curls bobbed. "Know who painted it?"

Gloria shook her head. Hank pointed to Will. "He did." The child's face lit with interest. "Know what else he painted?"

"What?"

"The picture in Mommy and Daddy's bedroom. The one of the river?"

Shit. Will recalled the painting. At least Sunny Sheldon had been telling the truth about selling his paintings to Melody.

Gloria straightened in her dad's arms. "Really?"

"Really. If you don't believe me, ask him."

Will's heart melted when the child shifted her blue gaze to him. "Really?"

"Cross my heart." He made an x across his chest with his index finger. "You like them?" When she nodded, he smiled. Leaning in close, he whispered, "Don't tell your mom, but she paid too much for them."

Hank's brows rose in question.

"Another long story best told over a bottle of cheap wine."

"You're on. Maybe this weekend? We've got a bunch of people coming in the following week to record. I could use a quiet night before all hell breaks loose."

"Hell!" Gloria chimed in.

"Shh!" Hank rolled his eyes. "Don't let your mom hear you say that word or I'll be sleeping in my office for a month."

"I won't, Daddy. Promise."

Hank shared a conspiratorial smile with Gloria. "That's my girl." He set her down. "Practice time is over. Which means?" he prompted.

"Snack time!" She took off like a flash, stopping in the doorway long enough to tell her daddy goodbye and blow him a kiss. Will was smitten.

"You're a lucky SOB."

Hank smiled. "Don't I know it." He motioned to the couch situated beneath Will's painting. "Have a seat?"

Will shook his head. "Nah. I actually came here to see your new PR person."

Hank frowned. "If you think you're going to steal her away, you better think again. She's doing a fantastic job for us, and we won't let her go without a fight."

Hand up like a stop sign, Will was quick to shut down his train of thought. "Hell, no. Just need to talk to her for a few minutes." Hoping Hank wouldn't ask him to elaborate, he went on. "Heard the drums and couldn't pass up the opportunity to see a musical genius at work."

"Takes after her grandpa Ravenswood." Hank's smile almost made it to his eyes. "It's a bit frightening, to tell you the truth."

"I bet." He could only imagine the responsibility Hank carried on his shoulders. By all accounts, Earl Ravenswood had been a musical prodigy. If Gloria inherited even half his talent, nurturing it without letting it consume her would be difficult. "Add her remarkable talent to our list of things to talk about over dinner."

Hank's smile was genuine this time. "You bet." He extended his hand, and the two shook again. "It's good to have you back, man. We missed you."

Will dipped his chin in acknowledgment. "It's good to be home."

MacKenzie's office was a few doors down from Hank's on the opposite side of the hallway. Her door was open, and light spilled out into the hall. Will recalled the soundproofed rooms, like Hank's office, didn't have windows. Which meant, the walls in her office were nothing more than studs and drywall. If he was going to maintain any privacy, he'd have to make sure they kept their voices down. Not an easy feat when he wanted to get right in her face and vent his frustrations at the top of his lungs.

Jake would be so much better at this, but his brother wasn't here, so it was up to him to get the answers. Raging at her probably wasn't the best way to go about it. He stopped, fisted his hands at his sides, took a deep breath then let it out, easing his fingers open at the same time. When he felt as calm as he was going to get, he stepped into the doorway and leaned against the frame. His stance said casual, but he'd no doubt the expression on his face said otherwise.

She was on the phone, but as soon as she saw him, she ended the conversation. After replacing the handset in its cradle, she tossed the pen she'd been holding onto the blotter, rocked back in her desk chair, and sighed. "You know."

It wasn't a question.

"I know." Why did she have to be so damn beautiful? Memories of what it felt like to be inside her, the little sounds she made when he hit the right spots, his name on her lips when she came—the emotion in her eyes the one time he'd allowed himself that intimacy. Her lies. It all twisted up in his gut, made him see red.

"I'm sorry—"

He straightened but kept his arms crossed over his chest, his fists curled into his armpits. He didn't want her platitudes. Couldn't care less about the answers Jake wanted. The hell with the paintings. They were crap anyway. He'd always known it, but faced with another betrayal, he could see the last few years with new clarity. The money didn't matter. The paintings mattered even less. There was only one question burning in his gut. "Cut the bullshit, Kenzie."

Her lips snapped shut. Her gaze dropped to the top of her desk. He advanced so he towered over her. "All I want to know is why? Why me? What the fuck did I ever do to deserve this?"

A single tear tracked down her cheek. "How did you find out?"

"Doesn't matter." He dropped his fists to her desk, leaned in so his voice wouldn't carry. This was between them. No one else. "Why, Kenzie?"

"I don't know." She looked up then. Her watery eyes did nothing to ease the rage inside him, threatening to erupt like a volcano. "I swear, I don't know."

"He didn't tell you anything?"

"No."

"Never said a word about his plans? Never dropped a hint about stealing a million dollars' worth of art?"

"No." She pressed those goddamn kissable lips of hers into a fine line.

"And I'm supposed to believe you? You were running PR for the gallery opening. You were sleeping with the bastard for Christ's sake. How could you not know?"

She snatched a tissue from a box tucked behind her computer monitor then dabbed at the corner of her eyes. It was no more than a moment, but she pulled herself together, squared her shoulders, and stared him down. "How could *you* not know? *You* were sleeping with Jessica, or had she gotten tired of being treated like a whore and moved on?"

Before Will could close his mouth and straighten, she'd pushed her chair back and run for the door. He caught a glimpse of her shoulder as she cleared the doorway, headed god only knew where.

Will collapsed onto her desk, his fingers digging into the edge of the wood surface. Dammit all to hell. The verbal barb she'd slung at him had hit dead center. He should have known what his girlfriend/agent was up to. Should have treated Jessica better than he had. She'd encouraged him to paint more, to become an assembly line, but he was the one who had thrown himself into the work until there was no time for anything else. He'd eaten sporadically, washed even less, and when she'd forced him to step away from his studio, he'd used her in much the same way he'd used MacKenzie those first few times they'd been together.

Fuck, MacKenzie was right. He'd brought it all on himself. Did his bad behavior make what Jessica and Cecil had done okay? Hell, no. But he was starting to understand why they'd done it.

Why?

He had his answer, and it wasn't a pretty one.

Because you're a dick.

The knowledge felt like smoldering cinders in his belly and fueled a new rage aimed at himself. There had only ever been one way to deal with his emotions. He needed to paint.

Shoving off her desk, he stalked out of the barn to his brother's truck. By the time he pulled into the driveway of his childhood home, his fingers ached from clenching the steering wheel like a lifeline.

It took him almost an hour to hang the new tarps he dragged from the back of his brother's truck and cover the floor with newspaper he'd found in a string-bound stack next to a garbage can. Only then did he squeeze paint onto his palette and pick up a brush.

He started with red. Bold, angry slashes he made no attempt to temper. When he ran out of red, he moved to black then bruising shades of blue, purple, and magenta.

He didn't have a plan. No idea what he was painting. His rage, his self-hatred had no shape, no physical form, yet it expressed itself nonetheless as a tangible, visual incarnation of himself. Broken. Miserable. Fucked.

When the paint ran out, he threw the palette at the tarp he'd desecrated then sank to his knees on the unforgiving concrete floor. Holding his head between his hands in a vise-like grip, the rage poured from his body in the form of tears.

He didn't know how long he'd sat there, but when Rick wrapped his arms around him and dragged him to his feet, his eyes were dry and his soul empty. He'd put it all on the cheap canvas tarps. Every last bit of himself.

"Come on, brother. You need to eat and sleep. Then you can tell me what the fuck you did to my new tarps."

He didn't argue. Let Rick help him into the house. He ate because his brother told him to, but the food had no taste. Later, he slept because he had no choice.

CHAPTER TWENTY

Kenzie cursed her choice of shoes for the day as she stalked across Hank and Melody's back yard. Damn spike heels. Who was she trying to impress anyway? No one around here dressed the way she did. This was fucking Texas, not New York. If she stayed here, she'd have to invest in a new shoe wardrobe. Maybe even a pair of cowboy boots. She imagined a pair she'd seen a few days ago. The embroidered yellow roses on them had caught her eye as she'd strolled past the store window. "Should have bought them then," she muttered to herself. If she'd been wearing them a few minutes ago she would have driven their pointed toe into Will Ingram's shin on her way out the door.

"Should have bought what?"

The feminine voice stopped Kenzie in her tracks. Where the hell had it come from? A quick glance around Hank and Melody's backyard provided her answer. Her boss's wife, book in hand, sat in a lawn chair beneath an ancient oak tree. Dressed in jeans and a BlackWing T-shirt Kenzie estimated to be as old as the tree, feet bare, the woman looked as if she didn't have a care in the world.

"Kick-ass cowgirl boots." She wobbled over to the cluster of lawn furniture. Bracing herself on the back of the nearest chair, she slipped her shoes off, sighing as her bare feet met the soft green lawn.

"They'd be more comfortable than those, but I'll warn you, they're hot as hell in the summer. Maybe you could compromise on some sandals?"

She envisioned kicking Will while wearing sandals. "Nope. Need something with some grit."

Mel's right eyebrow rose. "For?"

"Kicking someone?"

At the sound of a vehicle accelerating up the driveway, both women turned to look. "Would your someone be William Ingram?"

Kenzie closed her eyes and shook her head. When she opened them, the man and his truck were out of sight. "How did you guess?"

Mel shrugged. Marking her page with a scrap of paper, she set her book aside. "I can add two and two." She waved to the chair Kenzie was using to hold herself upright. "Have a seat."

Kenzie sat.

"Hank called to let me know he'd invited Will over for dinner later this week. He mentioned Will was here to see you. Seeing you huffing it across the lawn like a pack of hounds were on your heels, no pun intended then seeing Will drag racing up the drive—well, the conclusion was pretty easy."

"No woolgathering on your brain."

"Want to talk about it?"

"No. Not really." But it didn't stop her from telling Melody everything, starting with first seeing Will at JFK in New York and being attracted to him, to the accusations he'd thrown her way a few minutes ago. She left out a lot of details, but anyone with ears could have filled in the blanks, and Mel had two perfectly good ones.

"Does he know you're in love with him?"

Love. The word made her heart ache and her stomach churn.

"I told him. Sort of." *She's thinking how much she loves the man who put that expression on her face.* "But I don't think he believed me."

"Does he love you?"

"No!" She could still feel the heat of his anger as he accused her of lying. But maybe he had loved her, at least for a while. She'd seen it in his eyes, felt it in the way he claimed her the last few times they'd been together. What she'd seen and felt had been enough to make her rethink telling him everything. Another mistake to add to her mounting tally. "I think he hates me."

"Why would he hate you?"

"It's another long story, and I'm sure you've got things you need to be doing."

Mel shook her head. "Nope. Gloria is sound asleep. I brought the monitor out with me. If she wakes up, we'll hear her." She held up the romance novel she'd been reading. "And this can wait. I'd much rather hear about a real romance."

Kenzie's laugh held no mirth. "If you want romance, better stick to your book. Will hates me, and in his mind, he has good cause. Heck, I don't even blame him. I should have told him who I was as soon as I figured out who he was."

"And who are you, MacKenzie Carlysle?"

"I was involved in what happened to him in New York."

Mel adjusted in her seat. "There were a few articles about him in the local paper when it happened, but they were vague. Nothing since. I assumed it had all been resolved. How were you involved?"

She filled her new friend in on the particulars. No matter how she tried to spin it, the situation sounded bad.

"You're right. You should have told him."

"And you and Hank, too. Will is your friend. I don't want my employment to come between you."

"We knew some of your story. Sunny told us, but she didn't go into a lot of detail. She's a good friend, and we trust her judgement. However, I'll talk to Hank. See what he says. He's known the Ingram brothers his entire life. If you really didn't have anything to do with what happened to Will, then you working for BlackWing shouldn't be an issue."

"I swear I didn't know a thing about what Cecil and Jessica were up to. I was as surprised as anyone when I got to the gallery and found it empty."

Melody shifted in her seat. "I can't believe they stole the money *and* all the paintings. Who does something like that?"

Kenzie shook her head. "I can't tell you how many times I've asked myself the same question. How could I have been so stupid? I never saw it coming. I was working my ass off, doing PR for Will's showing and another one Cecil had scheduled a few months out. He never did or said anything to make me suspicious. It was business as usual, though, in hindsight, I can see how far he and I had drifted apart."

"It happens if you don't work at a relationship."

Nodding, Kenzie said, "Our relationship had broken down long before Cecil disappeared." She pressed her fingertips to her temples as old, painful memories came roaring to the forefront. "We argued a lot, mostly about him going out without me and coming home later than a guy with a woman waiting at home should. I know now he was with Jessica." Kenzie sighed and dropped her hands to her lap. "I was so stupid."

"You didn't want to see what was happening."

"No, I suppose I didn't. It was easier to pretend things weren't as they seemed. Deep down, I knew he was cheating on me, but I didn't know if it was one woman or a different one every night. I didn't *want* to know. So, I worked night and day and refused to look too closely at my personal life."

"Then he disappeared."

"Yeah. I had my own bank account where I kept my paychecks. Thankfully, he wasn't able to touch those funds—or maybe he didn't try—I didn't have much. But he cleaned out his personal accounts and the business accounts."

"Crazy things happen in the music and entertainment industries all the time, but your story beats anything I've ever heard."

"I landed on my feet, thanks to you guys and Sunny Sheldon. I was down to my last few dollars when I got here. I still had a credit card with some room on it, so I was able to survive." Just how she'd used some of her dwindling credit in the Philly airport warmed her blood. She'd been impetuous and more than a little stupid. If she'd known who the sexy stranger was, she never would have approached him, much less propositioned him. If she'd found an ounce of restraint, she wouldn't be in the predicament she was. She wouldn't be 100 percent, irrevocably in love with a man who hated her.

"What are you thinking?"

"Me?" Kenzie raised a hand to her cheek, felt the heat of her skin. "Nothing."

"Come on, girlfriend. You're blushing. What's going on?"

There was no use trying to argue the point. Her flaming cheeks had given her away. "Just remembering what it was like to be with him."

"Good, I take it?"

"Better than good. The best. He gets me. Did from the very first. It's not his fault I fell hard and he didn't."

"What makes you think he didn't fall, too?"

"You saw him spewing gravel to get away from here. He hates me."

Melody tapped her fingertips on the arm of her chair. "Haven't you heard? Love and hate are two sides of the same coin."

Kenzie's heart thumped hard. "You think he loves me?"

"I don't know, but I think it's highly likely. The deeper his feelings are for you, the bigger your betrayal would seem. Maybe he's trying to find a way to cope with the way he feels about you and the way he *thinks* he should feel about you."

Kenzie leaned back in the Adirondack chair and let her lids drop shut. "Betrayal." She mulled the word over in her mind. "I didn't betray him, but I can see how he would think I had. Not telling him about my involvement with Cecil was a mistake, but I did plan to tell him. I'd made my mind up to do it several times, but then we'd…well, let's just say we didn't do a lot of talking." She opened her eyes, studied the dappled light filtering through the leaves of the shade tree. "The time just never seemed right."

"Words aren't always necessary between two people."

Kenzie's laugh held no mirth. "Yeah, but trust is, and he doesn't trust me."

"I can't tell you what to do, but I know what it's like to love someone and be afraid to fight for him." Kenzie raised an eyebrow brow, and Mel continued. "I was stupid in love with Hank and because of my own fears, I almost let him get away. Be brave, Kenzie. If you love him, put on your big girl panties and go after him. Tell him what's in your heart. Beg him to listen to your side of the story. If he loves you, he'll find his way past the pain, and if he doesn't, maybe you can find peace in knowing you tried."

Leaning forward, Kenzie took Mel's hands in hers. "Thank you so much for listening to me today. You're right. Will is worth fighting for. I think we have a chance at something good, if I haven't ruined it."

Mel stood, and Kenzie rose with her. "I'm always here if you need someone to talk to, but now, if you'll excuse me, I should check on Gloria."

"Please, don't let me keep you."

"You haven't. I've enjoyed our talk. Feel free to stay a while. No one will bother you out here."

"Thanks. I think I will sit for a while. I know I need to face Will, but not before I figure out what I'm going to say."

"Take your time." When Mel reached the steps, she glanced over her shoulder. "My advice? Be direct. Men don't always understand subtlety."

With a wave and a genuine laugh, Kenzie dropped into her chair. She owed Will an apology, at the very least. Suggesting he in any way was responsible for what happened to him was beyond wrong. If Jessica felt like she'd been shorted in their relationship, she should have confronted him instead of conspiring with another man to destroy Will's career. She should have been direct.

Like I need to be. No more secrets. No more hiding my feelings or letting Will hide his. If he hates me, he needs to say so. Then we'll both know where we stand, and where we go from here.

CHAPTER TWENTY-ONE

Will cracked one eye open. Soft light spilled through the cheap vinyl blinds covering the single window in the small room. It was too early to be awake, especially since he didn't have a clue how long he'd been asleep. He vaguely recalled Rick helping him to stand. And he remembered the paint. So much goddamn paint.

The low rumble of voices coming from somewhere down the hall was what he needed to force his feet to the floor. Rick had called in reinforcements. A sure sign he'd fucked up—bad.

Will stumbled to the bathroom. Necessities first. Inquisition later.

After washing his hands, he dared a glance in the mirror over the vanity. He looked like he'd been to Hell and back. He splashed some cold water on his face which did nothing for his bloodshot eyes, but helped clear his head. He'd need his wits about him to face his brothers.

They knew he was up. The house was too small to conceal his movements. They could wait. After pulling on a T-shirt and sweats, he made his way to the kitchen, made a cup of coffee in Rick's fancy new one-cup brewer, and drank down half of it before heading to the living room to face the music.

"Thought you were in New York." He dropped into the only unoccupied chair in the room.

Jake adjusted the seams on his immaculate dress slacks. "I was. Rick called and said you had some sort of breakdown and I needed to get here ASAP."

Will sipped his coffee then stared at the remaining brew. "You should have stayed there."

"You aren't denying you had a breakdown."

"Nope. I hit bottom yesterday." Truth. He'd seen the depths of the pit and come back from it. Sort of. "I'm fine though." An enormous lie. He was far from fine, but his brothers would never leave him alone if they thought otherwise. "Just needed to work the toxins out of my system." If they believed his story, he should take up acting.

"Is that what we saw out there?" Rick gestured toward the garage. "Toxins?"

"You always were a Neanderthal when it came to art. That's a self-portrait, asshole."

"What the fuck?" Jake scooted to the edge of the sofa cushion. "Have you seen what you did? It looks like we let a madman loose in the garage."

Will held his older brother's gaze. "Fuck you."

"Look, Will," Rick appeased. "We're concerned about you. What you did out there yesterday isn't your normal technique."

"No, it's not. But it is the most honest thing I've ever painted." He jerked upright. "You didn't move anything, did you?"

"No. Jake just got here a few minutes ago. We weren't sure if we should leave it or throw it away before you woke up."

"Don't fucking touch it. You hear me?"

Jake held his hand up, palm out. "Okay. Calm the fuck down. We haven't, and we won't. It obviously means something to you."

He loved his brothers. He really did. But they would never understand what drove him to paint. Or not to paint. Just like he'd never understand how Jake could be happy wearing a suit and tie all day long, or how Rick could have joined the military. They physically resembled each other, but under their skin, they were as different as any three humans could be. "It means everything. Every. Fucking. Thing." He stood. "Come on. I'll show you."

The grass was cool under his bare feet as he led the way to the garage. He didn't expect them to truly understand, but he needed to convince them he hadn't lost his mind. Yeah, he'd been blind with rage and a host of other emotions he wasn't ready to pull out and examine in the light of day just yet, but he'd known what he was doing.

He thought he was ready to see it again, but standing there with the three huge canvases strung from the ceiling, reflecting his likeness back at him like a macabre three-sided mirror, was enough to freeze the breath in his lungs. His gaze swung from one panel to the next, assessing the technique, the message.

"Fuck, I'm good."

Jake stood to his left and just a little behind him. "If you say so. Looks like a mess to me."

"Me, too." Rick took up the same spot on his right side. "Explain, brother, before Jake and I have you committed."

He laughed, deep and loud. "It's a self-portrait. See." He pointed to the panel on the left. "Red. My life. My blood." He waved his hand to indicate the center panel. "Black. My soul."

"What about this one?" Rick faced the last tarp. "What the hell is this supposed to be?"

"My body. Purple for my heart, no disrespect to the military. Magenta, etcetera, for the rest of my organs."

"This is how you felt yesterday?" Jake stepped closer to look at the last panel. "Like you were a bunch of separate parts?"

Will nodded. "Yeah." He ran both palms over his face. "I'm surprised you picked up on it."

"I get more than you give me credit for, little brother. But this"—he got in Will's face and motioned to the walls of paint-splattered canvas—"is a bit frightening."

"I can see how you'd think so. Especially this one." He pointed to the first tarp. "It kind of resembles a crime scene."

"It's violent as fuck." Rick stared up at the slashes of red on beige backdrop. "What the hell were you thinking?"

"I wasn't suicidal or homicidal, if that's what you're asking."

"Good to know," Jake said.

"Have you ever looked at yourself and wished you could start completely over? New skin. New soul. New blood. New life?"

"Yeah." Rick's voice was a mere whisper, but there was truth behind the single syllable. Will should have been surprised, but he wasn't. He'd known Rick was hiding something from them, but he'd been too wrapped up in his own little world to question his brother. He made a mental note to let Rick know he was there for him if he needed anything. Anything at all. It was the least he could do for him, given how much Rick had done for him in the last few weeks.

"Then you might eventually understand. This is me." He swept his arm out to encompass the giant painting. "Bleeding out. Baring my soul. Hari-kari on canvas." He turned his back to the painting, held his arms out wide. "This is the new me. Starting over from scratch."

"What do you mean by starting over?"

Leave it to Jake to grab for something concrete. "I realized yesterday I've been a total shit for most of my life. I've thought of nothing but myself. I separated myself from my family and friends and let people who claimed to be friends but weren't rule my life. This"—he motioned to the still-wet tarps—"is the old me. Gone. I'm starting over. I'm going to paint what I want to paint, not what I think will sell. If I have to paint houses for a living, then so be it." He flashed a half-smile at Rick. "Maybe I can learn a few more things if you're willing to teach me. I'll work for apprentice wages—if you'll have me."

"Fuck, Will." Rick slapped him on the back. "You know I'll be more than happy to have you work with me. You've got a good eye." He pointed at Will's latest art work. "This, notwithstanding. I could use you, especially when it comes to design work."

"You're going to work construction?" Jake didn't even try to keep the skepticism out of his voice. "Seriously?"

"What? You're afraid you're going to have to support me?"

"No. You've got the money back they stole from you. You don't have to work manual labor if you don't want to."

"I want to. I thought I would hate it, but I don't."

Rick stepped between them. "Can we discuss something really important now?"

He'd snagged their attention. "My life isn't important?" Will asked.

"Not saying it isn't. I am wondering what the fuck I'm supposed to do with your self-portrait though. It can't hang here forever. I do use this garage, you know?"

"I was thinking about that. Can you make some big stretchers for me?"

Rick whistled low. "You're going to keep these?"

"Hell, yeah. I need to get them stretched before the paint completely dries. Otherwise, it's going to crack and peel off."

"*Then* what are you going to do with them?"

Will had wanted to do something like this for years, had thought Jessica would be the partner to help him make it happen. Yesterday, he'd realized he didn't need a partner. All he needed was himself. "I went out to Hank's place yesterday. You know how he converted the old barn into offices and a recording studio? I've wanted to do something similar for a long time. I told you about hunting for a place in upstate New York. Since I'm here to stay and I can't live with my baby brother forever, I was thinking of trying to find a farm for sale around here. Something with a barn I can convert to an art studio. I'll hang these on the walls for inspiration."

"Your own place isn't a bad idea." Jake smiled. "I think I might know a place, too."

"You're moving out?"

"Thought you wanted to get rid of me, little brother."

"Not you, just these scary as fuck paintings."

"I promise I'll take them with me." He turned his attention to Jake. "You know a place?"

"I handle a lot of estate work for people around these parts. Remember Bobby Hanover?"

Will searched his memory for the connection. "He was in your grade, right?"

"A year ahead of me. Anyway, his parents are both gone, left the family farm to him. He works for some big hotel chain, travels a lot. Wants nothing to do with the place. He's out of the country right now but said he was going to put it on the market as soon as he gets back. I could contact him, see what he wants for it. Bonus—it's next to my property. We'd be neighbors."

Will dug his phone out and pulled the property up on a popular real estate app. It had everything he wanted, a small house and a big barn that didn't appear too far gone in the photos. They discussed the particulars for a few more minutes then Jake left with a promise to contact the owner. Will was still exhausted, but he felt better than ever. The self-portrait had taken everything he had, mentally and physically, but it had been worth it. He was ready to put New York behind him and start his new life. One with more balance. One where he listened to his muse instead of telling it what to do.

"You ready to talk about the other painting?" Rick nodded at the draped easel stuffed in the corner. Jake hadn't seen it or he would have asked about it, too. The man couldn't help himself. He had to know everything.

Will shrugged. "What about it?"

"Are you going to show it to me? Or is it just going to take up space in my garage?"

He didn't know what he was going to do with it. He couldn't sell it, and the rightful owner didn't want it. "I'll take it with me when I go. Until then, it stays as is."

"What is it, a nude?"

Will's gaze snapped to his little brother.

"What?" Rick raised both eyebrows. "Really? And you aren't going to let me see?"

"Nobody sees it." He found the *I'll pound you into sand* voice he'd used on Rick when they were kids. "No. One. You got it?"

"Okay. Okay. I get it. No peeking."

Will stomped toward the door. "Got any food in this place? I'm starving."

CHAPTER TWENTY-TWO

For the second time in one week, Kenzie looked up from her desk to see one of the Ingram brothers standing in her doorway. She'd never met Jake Ingram, but the familial resemblance was unmistakable. This brother was perhaps a little taller than the other two, but, from the top of his head to his polished dress shoes, this one stood out. Jake's dark suit fit like it had been custom tailored to his broad shoulders and slim hips, physical attributions his brothers shared, but where Rick wore his mahogany hair in a military high-and-tight style, and Will went the other way, wearing his just a tad longer than the current fashion, this Ingram brother wore his hair neatly trimmed in a courtroom-appropriate style, as her father would say. And, like his brother before him, Jake Ingram didn't look particularly pleased to be there.

What now? She sighed and rocked back in her chair.

"A few minutes of your time." One long stride brought him in front of her desk. "I'm Jake Ingram."

"I know who you are." Throwing him out was beyond her abilities. She could call Hank or one of the tech guys working down the hall to assist her, but doing so would only draw attention to a situation she'd rather stay buried. Resigned to hearing him out, Kenzie waved to the chair in front of him. "Have a seat." Before his butt hit the chair, she repeated, "What do you want?"

Jake took his time adjusting his six-foot-plus frame into the tiny chair she'd inherited along with the office. Delay tactics designed to put the opponent on edge. Every lawyer had them. She should know. Her father stood at the top of the lawyer food chain, and he'd gotten there via his superior intimidation skills. Jake was good, but she'd faced down the best. *Get on with it.* She eyed the stack of press releases she still needed to edit and send out. The sooner he had his say, the sooner she could get back to work.

He made a show of straightening the creases in his suit pants then turned his *I'm in charge so don't even think of lying to me* expression on her. Oh, he was good, but compared to Sherman Carlysle, Jake Ingram was a teddy bear. "I'm here on behalf of my brother, William, who also happens to be my client."

"Is your brother planning to sue me?"

"No." He frowned. "Why would he sue you?"

"I don't have any idea." She leaned forward, picked up her discarded pen, and twirled it between her fingers. "But it's the only reason I can think of for you to be here."

Jake cleared his throat. "Well, actually, I came to ask you a few questions."

Though she knew the answer, she asked anyway—couldn't be too careful around lawyer types. She'd learned early on to understand exactly what was being asked and make sure her answer gave nothing else away. "About what?"

"About your relationship with Cecil Hawthorne and your possible involvement in the theft of my brother's paintings."

"My relationship with Cecil Hawthorne is none of your business, and I did not have anything to do with the theft of Mr. Ingram's paintings."

"Will said as much—about the paintings. But I beg to differ on the subject of your relationship with the man who did steal the artwork."

Will told him she didn't steal his paintings? Something inside her broke at his admission. Maybe he didn't hate her after all. *Not* hate wasn't love, but it was *something*. As much as she wanted to help recover the stolen art, she didn't see how anything she knew could be of help. Still.... She owed Will her complete cooperation. It wouldn't change anything between them, but she could answer a few questions. "I told the police everything I knew. I'm afraid it wasn't much. I was as shocked as anyone when I arrived to find the gallery empty." As the words spilled from her mouth, she wondered how many times she was going to have to say them in her lifetime. Would people still be talking about this case when she was old and gray?

"The police weren't overly concerned with locating the paintings. No one even filed missing person reports on Mr. Hawthorne or Ms. Blackwell. They're listed as persons of interest in the reports, so no effort was made to actually locate them."

"No one reported either of them missing?" She'd been so furious and hurt, she hadn't cared where the two of them had gone, but surely a family member had reported them missing by now. "Oh. Are you saying someone knows where they are?"

"I'm thinking it's highly likely someone does. Otherwise, missing person reports would have been filed on them by now, wouldn't you think?"

There was no mistaking the accusation in his voice. Kenzie straightened her shoulders. "Are you insinuating *I* know where they are? Because, if you are, you can get the hell out of my office right now."

"Simmer down, Ms. Carlysle. I'm not insinuating you know anything. I am saying, it's highly likely one or more of their family members know where they are."

"Yet, you're here asking me about them. Why aren't you asking their relatives?"

"Because it's also highly unlikely a relative would give them up."

"I told you, I don't know where Cecil went."

Jake nodded. "I believe you. However, I think you might have information that could lead me to them."

Kenzie shook her head. "I told you. I don't know anything. Cecil and I hardly saw each other for weeks before he disappeared. We talked even less."

"You were handling his business affairs."

"Yes. I was. To an extent. I didn't have access to any of the financial accounts. I could deposit, but not withdraw funds. I sorted his mail. Answered inquiries about the gallery and upcoming openings. It was my job. I did PR for the gallery."

"I don't expect you to remember anything right away, but think back, if you will? Did you see anything come for him from a Realtor or take a phone message from one? Maybe an email you saw or deleted thinking it was spam?"

"You think he's still in the country?"

"I don't know. Perhaps. Unless they stole money from someone other than my brother, they didn't get enough to start a new life abroad, at least not a comfortable one. Even if they did leave the country, I doubt they would have taken the paintings with them. Better to let them cool off for a while then ship them a few at a time. Did Mr. Hawthorne have a storage unit?"

"He did, but I had a key to it. The police checked. It was empty."

"What did he store there?"

"Stuff for the gallery. Pedestals, chairs, tables, tools for hanging paintings. Paint cans. The usual stuff."

"Was it cleaned out, or were those things still there?"

"It was cleaned out. Completely empty."

"Didn't it strike you as odd that he would dispose of mundane items such as you described?"

Had she thought it odd? "I don't recall thinking about it at all. I was in shock, Mr. Ingram. I'm sure I wasn't thinking clearly at the time."

"Which is exactly why I want you to think about it now. Don't force the memories, just let them come. Please, write down anything you remember, even if you don't think it's important. Odd phone calls, emails, letters. Did he take any trips out of town? Or disappear for any length of time you couldn't account for?"

Kenzie scoffed. "He was gone a lot. I couldn't possibly account for his whereabouts with any certainty."

"All I'm asking you to do is try to remember. Any tidbit of information, no matter how insignificant it might seem, could lead me in the right direction."

She didn't want to think about Cecil or what he'd done, but she would. For Will. Before she could think better of it, she asked, "How's your brother?"

Jake's left eyebrow arched. "Why do you ask?"

Damn lawyer. They were all nosy as hell. "Because he was pretty angry when he left here yesterday." She paused, swallowing her pride hard. "I didn't mean to upset him."

Will's brother stared at her until she began to fidget in her seat. "He's been better. He painted all night long."

Kenzie jerked her gaze to his. "He painted?"

"If you could call what he did painting. Looks like mayhem with a paintbrush to me, but he claims it's a self-portrait."

Kenzie felt her heart sink to her toes. "I might have said some things to him...."

"You think?" Jake stood. "I don't know what is going on between you two, but it's got him tied up in knots."

"I'm sorry."

"Don't be. As scary as his latest painting is, at least he's showing emotion. I don't know if getting the stolen art back will help or not, but I'm going to try."

"I'll think about those last few months. If I come up with anything, I'll let you know."

Jake reached into his pocket, drew out a leather card case. He tossed a business card on her desk. "Call me anytime. My cell number is on there as well as my office number."

"Jake."

At the sound of her voice, he turned, his hand on the doorjamb. "What?"

She didn't know why, but, suddenly, she felt the need to come clean with Will's brother. Before she could talk herself out of it, she blurted, "I'm in love with your brother."

With a faint nod to acknowledge her words, Jake continued on his way.

The sound of her desk phone ringing made her nearly jump out of her skin. After a quick deep breath, she picked up the handset. "MacKenzie Carlysle. How may I help you?"

Thanks to the phone call from the tour organizer, Kenzie didn't have a single minute to think about anything but work for the remainder of the day. Adding an extra show at five of their locations required immediate attention to ensure ticket sales wouldn't disappoint. She'd spent the rest of the day working to get the word out. By the time she pulled into her driveway, she wanted nothing more than to crawl under the covers and forget the day had ever happened, but as soon as she saw the work Rick had completed while she was at work, the visit from Jake Ingram popped into her mind and refused to go away.

The rain that had kept Will from working outside was the perfect backdrop for an evening revisiting one of the darkest periods of her life. Curled up on the sofa with a microwaved dinner and a bottle of wine, Kenzie let her thoughts roam to her time with Cecil.

Things had been good at first. He'd been a good boss, and soon after starting to work for him, he'd become an attentive lover. She'd been too shocked by his betrayal to examine the breakdown of their relationship too closely. She'd told the police they'd drifted apart, but was there more to the story?

The job at the gallery had been her first real job, and she'd worked hard to prove she was up to the task of promoting an established art gallery. She'd never once wondered why Cecil had hired her instead of one of the more qualified applicants, of which there had been many.

She'd seen for herself when he'd left the applications for her to file. Several had experience with even larger galleries than Hawthorne's. The job should have gone to one of them. But he'd hired her. Then wooed her into his bed a few weeks later.

Sipping her wine and listening to the rain patter on the roof, she tried to look at the broader picture. Had Cecil been planning something even then? Had he hired her because of her inexperience? Because he knew she wouldn't question his actions or realize something was wrong? It was a possibility she hadn't considered before.

Had she been the perfect pawn in a crazy scheme to take W.H. Ingram down? Had she unwittingly played right into Cecil's plans? Had she been stupid, naïve, or just plain snookered?

All of the above.

She'd been played. When she'd asked about her predecessor, Cecil had told her the man had decided to retire outside the city to be close to his grandkids. He'd apparently worked for Cecil for almost a decade. What was his name? Kenzie clutched her wineglass to her breast and closed her eyes, willing the name to come back to her. She'd seen it dozens of times her first few months on the job as she slowly took up the PR reins he'd dropped.

What was it? What was it? Robert. Ronald. Roland. Ross. "Ross something." *It was something Scottish, like MacKenzie.* "McClelland! Ross McClelland!" He'd moved upstate somewhere. She searched her brain for any scrap of memory regarding his new location and came up empty. There had to be a record though. Cecil's accountant would have sent tax information to the man.

It wasn't much, but it was a lead. Ross had worked for Cecil a lot longer than she had. Maybe he knew things. Maybe it was the reason he'd retired.

I need to call Jake.

Kenzie grabbed her cell phone from the coffee table then stopped. Where was the card Jake had given her? *Fuck.* It was on her desk. Buried beneath a week's worth of work still waiting for her. Refusing defeat, she opened an Internet browser. Within seconds, she had a number for Jake Ingram, Attorney at Law. If he was anything like her father, he put in ridiculous hours at the office. She might just catch him there.

After three rings, she got his voicemail. She listened to the usual list—office hours—leave a message. She was about to hang up when the recorded voice added, "If this is an emergency, call 555-1619."

Was it an emergency? No. She didn't need someone to bail her out of jail, but she did want Jake to know she was taking her assignment seriously. Hanging up, she dialed his emergency number.

"Jake Ingram."

"Jake, this is MacKenzie Carlysle. I hope I'm not disturbing you."

CHAPTER TWENTY-THREE

He should get an acting award. He'd snowed his brothers good. They actually thought he'd gotten his shit together. Truth? He was knee-deep in excrement of his own making. Rick had ordered lumber to build the giant stretchers for his self-portrait, the one thing he hadn't lied about, and Jake was looking into property for him to purchase. So, maybe he hadn't lied about spending his money on real estate, either. A house was as good a place as any to invest the funds Jake had recovered. If he'd invested the money he'd made early on when he'd been putting his heart and soul into his paintings instead of squirreling the money away in a standard savings account, Jessica wouldn't have been able to get her hands on every dime. After all this time, he still couldn't believe the amount some of his paintings had sold for. Enough to establish him as a major player in the art world.

Then he'd met Jessica and let her persuade him to paint for the masses. The paintings were good, but, unlike his early work, he hadn't put an ounce of himself into any of them. They sold like snow cones on a summer day, and he'd painted more. The canvases destined for the gallery showing had been worth a small fortune in terms of money, but in art terms, they were emotionless, lifeless crap. Admitting he'd painted crap to feed his bank account hurt like hell, but it was a truth he needed to learn to live with. He'd put more of himself into the nude hidden in the garage and the self-portrait than anything else he'd painted in years. Hell, he'd put more of himself into painting Kenzie's house than he'd put into all the paintings her boss and his girlfriend had stolen.

He'd been motivated by greed. If future art historians even recalled his name, they'd probably dub his time with Jessica as his commercial period. He'd forever think of it as his asshole period. Take that Van Gogh!

Nevermore. If he couldn't make a living selling genuine paintings, he'd slap paint on houses during the day and indulge his muse at night. From now on, he planned to be one thing—authentic. He'd go back to his roots and paint from his heart. Dig down deep in his soul and put his emotions on canvas.

Thanks to a Texas-sized rainstorm, he'd had nothing but time on his hands for the last few days. Rick had offered to show him a few building techniques indoors, but Will had begged off. The last place he wanted to be right now was inside Kenzie's house. He'd borrowed Rick's truck again and made a trip into Dallas for art supplies. He brought a few canvases home with him and arranged for more to be delivered. There was nothing worse than needing to sling paint and having nowhere for it to go. Witness his self-portrait done on paint tarps.

Standing in the garage, listening to the rain on the roof and staring at a blank canvas, Will didn't know what he'd been thinking when he bought the new easel and stack of canvases. He only had one image in his head and it was one he couldn't shake.

MacKenzie Carlysle.

Every time he picked up a paintbrush, all he wanted to paint was her. When he tried to sleep, he dreamed of her. Scorching-hot dreams he feared were actual memories he had no hope of erasing from his mind. Waking from one such dream, Will kicked the sheet aside but refused to take himself in hand to ease the never-ending ache for her. Instead, he did what he always did—thought of the last time he'd seen her.

He'd accused her of all manner of things. Found her guilty by association alone. He'd hurt her with his words, but not nearly as much as he'd hurt her with his actions. Recalling her words as she'd left him standing in her office was enough to extinguish the fire burning inside him every time.

"How could you not know? You were sleeping with Jessica, or had she gotten tired of being treated like a whore and moved on?"

He owed MacKenzie about a dozen apologies. One for every time he'd fucked her then left as if she didn't matter in the least. Several more for thinking then accusing her of any involvement in what Jessica and Cecil had done to him. He owed her an apology for dismissing the love she'd all but confessed when he'd shown her the painting. The love he, himself, had captured for all time when he'd painted her.

Suddenly, he realized what he needed to paint. No need to sketch it first. He knew every line, every shadow, every curve of her face.

"Hey."

Will jerked his hand away from the canvas and spun toward the source of the interruption. Rick stood in the open doorway, rain dripping from the eaves behind him. Seeing it was only his brother, he raised his brush again and contemplated the exact spot where it should touch down. "What? Aren't you supposed to be at the jobsite?"

His brother's gaze darted from the rafters to the floor to his hand gripping the doorframe. "I'm taking the rest of the day off." He swallowed hard. "Friend of mine is going to be in town. Dallas. I'm going to go see him."

Will lowered the brush again and looked at his brother. As far as he knew, Rick hadn't left Willowbrook since the day he'd returned home from his stint in the Marines. He hadn't socialized with any of his old friends and never mentioned any he'd made during his enlistment. He looked nervous as a teenager caught skipping class and...he was taking a day off work. "A Marine buddy?"

"Yeah. Haven't seen him in a while."

"How long's he going to be in town?"

"Just passing through. Flight delay."

Will chuckled. "Know all about them. I'm sure he'll be glad for the distraction." He side-eyed the painting-in-progress. *Best airport distraction ever.* Not everybody could be as lucky as him—like the poor Marine who would have Rick for company. His brother never was much of a talker. These days he rarely said anything.

"I-I'll probably just spend the night."

"Okay. Don't worry about me. I'll be fine."

"If you get a chance, Ms. Carlysle asked if you could start painting the inside of her house since this rain doesn't look like it's going to stop anytime soon."

Will closed his eyes against the jolt of awareness shooting through him at the mention of her name. If he timed it right, he could get the work done while she was at her office. He wasn't ready to see her yet. But Rick had agreed to the job, and Will worked for Rick now. He'd just have to suck it up and do what he needed to do. "Yeah. Did she decide on paint colors?" His dick hardened, recalling the night he'd taken the color palette over to her house. They'd gotten a lot done, but it had nothing to do with paint selections.

"Yep. Bought some, too. Paint cans are in the rooms they go in. Everything else you'll need is in the kitchen. Wants you to start on her bedroom."

Shit. She was trying to torture him. Made perfect sense, given the things they'd said to each other the last time he'd seen her. "Got it. Start in the bedroom." He dropped his brush into a jar of cleaner. "I'll go over after lunch and get started."

"Should be home before lunch tomorrow."

Will kicked the leg of his dad's old workbench. "Fuck." By the time he'd cleaned up and eaten a sandwich on stale bread, he'd forgotten all about Rick's strange behavior. Foremost on his mind was screwing up the courage to walk down the street. *She's at work. Just go in. Do the work and get the heck out before she comes home.*

He knew her usual schedule—set an alarm on his phone for a half hour earlier than she'd ever returned home while he'd been working on her house—then set out to paint. Walls.

Honest work, he reminded himself.

She'd chosen a pale blue for her bedroom. As he moved furniture to the center of the room and covered it with plastic sheeting, he thought she'd done a good job of coordinating her bedding and window treatments with the wall color. The blue would anchor the white comforter and pick up the pattern in the curtains still in their packaging. The completed room would have a classic look. Like the way she dressed.

Did she want the inside of the closet painted, too? He peeked at the interior. The white walls had yellowed with age and were scuffed where shoes and such as had been tossed inside over the years. Yeah, she'd want the closet painted. Which meant her clothes had to go.

It was mostly work clothes, he decided, as he hauled armloads of sexy-as-hell suits to the adjacent bedroom and dropped them on the bed. Resting on the top of the last bundle was the suit she'd had on the day he confronted her in her office. He'd been furious. Beyond seeing straight, but he'd noticed her clothes. Noticed everything about her. She'd worn a soft, cream-colored blouse beneath the hunter-green jacket with a matching pencil skirt. He could still see her ass, perfectly delineated by the fabric as she'd stormed out of the office. Her calves, elongated by the fuck-me heels she'd had on were permanently etched in his brain.

Body parts. He loved body parts. Particularly women's. Calves. Breasts. Fingers. Shoulders. Loved how they all fit together to make a unique work of art. No two were alike, but in his eyes, they were all beautiful. MacKenzie Carlysle, however, put all the others to shame.

His fingers itched for a pencil or charcoal. Anything to record the image playing through his mind like the best porn ever. Running his fingers over the expensive fabric one more time, committing the texture to memory, he went in search of pencil and paper. Fuck the walls. They could wait.

CHAPTER TWENTY-FOUR

As soon as Rick Ingram called to say he was taking the rest of the day off to visit a friend, casually mentioning his brother had promised to get started on the inside painting this afternoon, Kenzie had begun to plan. She'd put in extra hours the last few days and was caught up enough to take a few hours off.

Fortunate to work for a boss who didn't care if she took time off as long as the work got done, she powered down her computer and recorded a *how to reach me in an emergency* message for her office phone. There were rarely emergencies in her line of work, but when one came up, it had to be dealt with posthaste or things could go sideways. She'd put too much work into BlackWing's upcoming tour promo to let something muck it all up. No matter what she had planned for the next twelve hours or so, she would only be a phone call away if disaster happened.

There was no one to save her if things went sideways at her house, which was highly likely. She was starting at rock bottom with William H. Ingram. Their relationship had begun at a crisis point for both of them, sped headlong into entanglement before it hit the median dividing their lives.

She'd said awful things to him the day he'd come to her office wearing his heart on his sleeve, not blaming her, only asking, why? She didn't have an answer for him, so she'd struck back, put the burden for everything their former lovers had done to him square on his shoulders.

It wasn't one of her better moments. She had a lot to answer for.

WILL

The house was silent as a tomb. Accustomed to hearing the music Rick kept on while he worked, she'd expected Will to do the same. Which meant the bastard hadn't shown up to paint the way he'd said he would. Frustrated, she stood just inside the front door, wondering if she should go to the office or stay home. Everything she needed to paint the walls was here, and she could search the Internet for instructions. Despite her decision not to pursue a law degree the way her dad had wanted, she wasn't a dummy. She could learn to paint.

Fuck Will Ingram. I'll do it myself.

Kenzie dropped her briefcase and purse on the sofa, stuffed her cell phone in the back pocket of her new jeans then went in search of old clothes to paint in. Determination or not, she wasn't stupid enough to believe she could paint without getting as much on her as she put on the walls.

Nearing the first, and smallest, of the two bedrooms, a slight sound caught her attention. Mice? God, she hoped not. Stopping to listen, she heard it again. Not mice then, which meant someone else was in the house. Creeping as much as her new western boots allowed, she made her way down the hall and peeked around the corner. Will Ingram sat on the floor in her spare room, a crude board against his raised knees, sheets of paper he'd no doubt lifted from the stack she kept next to the home printer on the living room shelf. The floor surrounding him was littered with discarded drawings. Next to his right hip sat the earthenware coffee cup holding the pencil collection she'd started as a child. If she wasn't mistaken, the writing implement currently in Will's hand bore the name and address of Sunny Sheldon's gallery in Manhattan. Her friend would be pleased to see the inexpensive advertising had made it all the way to Texas. Even more pleased to know an artist of Will's caliber was using it to draw...what, exactly?

He didn't seem to know she was there. Brow crinkled in concentration, Will focused entirely on whatever he was drawing at the time. Kenzie edged around the corner, leaned against the jamb, arms and legs crossed in a casual pose. How many people could say they'd watched the process of a world famous artist? Not many. She was one of the lucky ones, luckier still to be the subject of all his concentration, for, as she focused in on some of the discarded sheets of computer paper, his subject matter became clear. They were all drawings of her. Sitting behind her desk. Walking out her office door. Bent over the table in her kitchen. Looking up at him on the ladder outside her house. They were crude, mostly just lines to suggest a pose, but with enough detail to be unmistakable to someone who had been in those positions.

What the hell is he doing? She was about to ask when he tossed another drawing onto the floor and reached for another blank page. "Don't fucking move."

Then the pencil was flying across the page. "Where'd you get the jeans?" He didn't so much as pause as he flung the question at her.

"Um. There's a store in Fort Worth. Cathy told me about it." She'd stocked up on jeans and dressy-but-practical cotton blouses to go with the boots she'd purchased at the store over on Main Street. In New York, suits had been the attire of choice for women in the workplace. Not so much here, and, after a few days wearing casual clothes to the office, she was beginning to see the benefit of dressing down. Suits required rigid posture, which, in turn, required energy to maintain. The last few days, she'd come home less fatigued than ever before. Then there was the dry cleaning bill she wouldn't miss.

Kenzie glanced at the pile of clothes on the bed Will leaned against. She'd keep some of the suits for business meetings and those rare trips to New York Hank had warned her about. She'd find a place to donate the remainder. Maybe one of those places where they helped women dress for job interviews and new careers. Her mother had supported one in D.C. for years.

"Unbutton the jeans."

Her gaze snapped back to Will. "What?"

"Do it. Now. Unbutton your jeans. Slide the zipper down."

He was insane, but she did it anyway.

"Fold the sides back. Let me see your panties then put your hands behind you. Yeah, perfect. Don't move."

Another drawing joined the stack on the floor as he grabbed another sheet of paper and began to draw. "What are you doing?"

"Drawing, what does it look like?"

"You were supposed to be painting my bedroom."

"And you're supposed to be at work."

She shrugged. "I came home early to talk to you."

Silence broken only by the scratch of pencil on paper stretched between them. Her fingers were going numb pressed between her ass and the doorjamb. After what seemed like a lifetime, he tossed another drawing aside and reached for another sheet of paper.

"Keep your left hand behind you. Slide your right one inside your panties. Not too far. Perfect."

Yep. I'm insane, she thought as his gaze roamed over her before he bent to his task. She'd never seen him like this, and she had to admit, Will Ingram in full-artist mode was sexy as hell. Trying to forget her fingers were brushing her bare mound, she focused on him instead. His hair was longer than when she'd first seen him, and it had been longer than current fashion then. A couple days stubble covered his jaw, and he'd clearly not spent any time shaping it up. No, he'd simply forgotten, or chose not to shave. God, how she'd love to feel his scruff against her skin. *Don't go there.* Just because she was posing for him didn't mean they'd settled anything. She'd come to talk to him, so talk she would.

"I'm sorry about what I said to you the other day."

"No need," he said, his hand still flying across the page. "You were right."

"No, I wasn't. None of this was your fault. You were the victim. It wasn't right to blame you."

"Forget it, Kenzie. It's done. Jessica and Cecil can go fuck themselves."

"I can't help feeling responsible. I should have known something was up. I was too caught up in my own misery at the time to think clearly."

"Didn't help that the police hardly asked you anything."

"No, it didn't. My dad might have had something to do with the light interrogation."

"Your dad, the attorney general?"

"You know?"

He nodded. "Jake told me."

She should have known his brother would want to know why the police had dismissed her involvement almost from the get-go. She'd made the mistake of calling her mother, the only parent who had encouraged her to find her own way in the world. Within minutes, her dad, the attorney general of the United States had spoken with someone in New York. A heartbeat later she'd been cleared of any involvement. The questions had stopped immediately. "Did he also tell you I gave him a name to chase down? Cecil's former PR guy?"

"He told me." *Skritch. Scratch.* "He's on his way to New York as we speak." *Skritch. Scratch.* "Doesn't matter though. I don't want the paintings back."

She gasped. "What? Why?"

"They're crap. I hope they burned them. Save me the trouble."

"You don't mean that."

"I do." Another drawing slid across the floor. A clean sheet of paper took its place on his crude lap board. "Use your left hand to unbutton your blouse. Just a couple of buttons. Yes. Perfect. Now slide your fingers inside your bra. Make your nipple hard."

"Will."

"Just do it, Kenzie."

She did.

"Slide your right hand down more. Find your heat and stay there. Chin down. Drop your eyelids. Not too much, slumberous. Yes, perfect. Lips parted. Damn, you're so natural. Perfect."

Skritch. Scratch.

She'd been naked with the man, but standing like this, fully clothed, she felt more exposed than ever. Her heart beat like a hammer behind her left palm, and the fingers of her right hand were wet. So damn wet. Her clit throbbed. Will barely spared her a glance then bent to his work. All focused concentration while she was dying a slow death against a doorjamb in sore need of a fresh coat of paint. In an effort to distract her thoughts from the sorry state of her body, the need pulsing through her, she forced her mind to think of something else.

This had been her boss's room when he was a boy. Some of the grimy handprints on the jamb were probably his. And some could be Will's. They'd been boyhood friends. Had spent time in each other's houses. They weren't boys anymore. They were full-grown men, and my, hadn't they turned out well? Hank was gorgeous. Talented beyond belief, but he did nothing for her. Not even a twinge of interest there.

But Will? He was another story altogether. She'd wanted him from the first moment she'd laid eyes on him. She hadn't known who he was. Didn't care. She'd simply known she had to have him, even if it was just one time. It should have been enough. But it wasn't. She'd never get enough.

"Just a little longer. Now, touch yourself. Make it feel good. But don't come. Not yet."

She didn't think about what she was doing as she uncrossed her ankles, spread her legs, and shoved her hand deeper between her legs to do as he said. One finger wasn't enough. She pushed a second then a third inside her tight channel. Her thumb brushed her clit. Again. And again.

"Don't fucking come." *Skritch. Scratch.* "Not until I tell you to."

"Will. Please."

CHAPTER TWENTY-FIVE

She was fucking killing him. He'd thought her sexy in her fancy business suits. But those jeans. And those fucking boots. When she'd leaned against the doorframe, it had been all he could do to remain where he was and not go to her.

They needed to talk. He had been avoiding her for days because he couldn't keep his hands off her. Sketching turned out to be his salvation. He could talk and sketch. And look his fill while doing so.

He'd never sketched so fast, but he needed to record the basics of what he was seeing. He'd never forget the way she was right that minute—leaning against a doorjamb, busy getting herself off for him. Goddamn, the image would be in his brain for the rest of his life. It was the fine details—the way her blouse draped around the hand inserted inside it. The folds of her jeans where she'd inadvertently pushed them lower on her hips to accommodate her other hand. The angle of her legs, spread to allow access to her core. He might get those right from memory, but he couldn't be certain he would, not when every molecule of his being was focused on the expression on her face and the little moans and breathless gasps coming from her mouth. Her very kissable, fuckable mouth.

The woman was his Kryptonite. She destroyed him with a look. With his name on her lips. With her very being.

Fuck the sketch. He'd have to rely on his memory.

Tossing aside the slab of plywood he'd found in the trash pile Rick had yet to remove from the kitchen, Will got to his feet. A second later, he stood before her, his fingers gripping her waist. "Don't stop."

"Will."

He didn't miss the plea in her voice. He understood her need all too well. He was hurting, too.

"Ken. Baby." Then his mouth was on hers, his lips moving, devouring hers, his tongue tasting, promising as he matched her fingers below, thrust for thrust. Touching her was pure heaven. Her body was a perfect match to his. Her need, her desire equal to his.

The need to dominate, to have her submit to him, to claim her, had been there from the beginning.

Skimming the outside of her blouse, he brushed his thumbs over the gentle swells of her breasts. He covered the one she hadn't been able to reach and squeezed. She broke their kiss, a groan escaping her lips. So fucking perfect. He couldn't take it another second.

As he tugged her hands from their duties, her eyes popped open, a question and a protest written in their depths. Gazes locked, he brought her wet fingertips up to his mouth, sucked her essence from them. "Turn around." The vulnerability in her gaze nearly broke him. "I won't leave you this time. Promise. I just need to do this to you. With you."

Every breath she took brought her breasts in contact with his chest as she looked into his eyes, searching for the words she needed from him. Words she deserved.

"After, Ken. Give me this then I'll give you what you want."

To his everlasting relief, she spun in his arms to face the doorjamb. He pressed his front to her back until there was no place for her to go. Skimming his hands from her shoulders to her wrists, he threaded his fingers through hers, stretching their arms above her head on either side of the jamb. With a flex of his hips, he drove hers up against the unforgiving wood.

He ducked his head, flicked out his tongue to taste a drop of sweat trickling from behind her ear down her neck. The salty flavor melded well with the lingering sweetness of her juices on his tongue. She smelled like sunshine, inexplicable on this cloudy, rainy day. *She'll always be my sunshine. The light at the end of my tunnel.*

He sucked in another lungful of her then brushed his lips over the shell of her ear and breathed out. "Fuck the doorjamb, Ken. Make yourself come right here. Right now."

She tensed for the span of a heartbeat then her hips began to move. "Perfect, baby. Fuck it. Get yourself off." His words were nasty, just the way she liked them. Finding her rhythm, he flexed his hips against her ass, driving her up and hard, making sure she found the contact, the pressure she needed to get off. "God, baby, you're fucking making me jealous of a piece of wood. Fuck it good, baby. Grind it."

Her fingers tightened in his grip. Her movements became erratic as she chased her orgasm. When it hit, a sob broke from her lips as she shamelessly rode the doorframe into ecstasy. He held her pinned there until spent, she sagged in his arms.

"So fucking beautiful, Ken. I've got to have you."

"Yes."

His arms full of woman, Will stood looking down at the only bed in the house he had any intention of using. The one in the other room wasn't near big enough for what he had in mind. "Fuck." He didn't want to put Kenzie down, but the plastic he'd thrown over her bed had to go.

"I've got it. Dip me down."

He bent his knees until she was able to grab a corner of the plastic. Walking backwards while she tugged, they managed to uncover the mattress.

"We're good together."

"No argument there." He tossed her to the center of the bed then grabbed one of her feet. "Nice boots but they've got to go." Yanking on the heel, he pulled until her foot popped free. After repeating the process with her other foot, he reached for the waistband of her jeans then stopped.

"Turn over. Let me see your ass in these jeans." She rolled over without argument. Propped on her elbows, she glanced over her shoulder. "Like what you see?"

He'd thought her ass perfect in those pencil skirts she favored, but that was before he saw her in a pair of jeans. She'd tempt a saint to sin, and he was far from sainthood. "Fucking hell, woman. You aren't going out in public in these, are you?"

"Of course I am, why?"

"Because I'm going to have to murder a hell of a lot of people for looking at what's mine."

"Yours?"

He raised one eyebrow.

"Okay, yours, but I'm still wearing them to work. They're comfortable."

He growled. Actually growled, which made the damn woman laugh as she flipped onto her back. They'd discuss her wardrobe choices another time.

"As spectacular as your ass is in these, they have to go, too."

"Then, by all means." She planted her bare feet on the mattress and lifted her hips. Hooking his fingers in the waistband, he tugged them past her hips then grabbed the hem of both legs to pull them the rest of the way off, leaving her bare from the waist down except for a fucking pair of white, lace-trimmed boy-short style panties he'd only caught a glimpse of before.

"Fuck, Ken."

A single finger traced the lace spanning her hips. "Like these, too?"

"You know I fucking do. But they've got to go. I need to see all of you."

"Not until you tell me."

Will ducked his head. Hands on his hips, he studied the toes of his shoes. He'd promised to give her the words she needed. Hell, he needed to say them. He just didn't know if he could, not with barriers between them. "Not like this." He kicked off his shoes then grabbed his T-shirt and yanked it over his head. His pants were next, along with his socks and underwear. "Naked. Nothing between us, Ken."

She looked at him like he was a piece of candy and she'd been on a decade-long diet. "Okay. But you promised. You aren't trying to distract me, are you?" She licked her bottom lip, and his dick throbbed.

Will groaned. "No. Trust me. I need to be inside you. And you need to feel me, too. There's nothing but truth when we're together."

Without further argument, she wiggled out of her panties then sat up to remove her blouse and bra. He stood, watching her practiced movements, not meant to tease but driving him insane anyway. Then she scooted up to the headboard, lay back, and spread her legs in invitation.

"Christ, Ken."

He was on her, in her before he drew his next breath. Her legs closed around his hips, anchoring him in place while her arms encircled his neck. Will lowered himself until they were pressed together from chest to groin. One.

Keeping as much weight as possible on his forearms, he cradled her face in his palms, brushed her cheekbones with his thumbs. He'd never felt this kind of connection with another human being. Never felt like he'd come home when he'd coupled with a woman. Never wanted to stay right where he was for the rest of his life. The thought was daunting, but there it was. She made him want to be the man she thought he was. He gazed into her eyes, and the words he feared he'd never be able to say tumbled from his lips.

"I've been an ass. A friggin' moron. I said things I didn't mean. I used you. Hurt you. I can't tell you how sorry I am for all of it. Not for fucking you blind at the airport. I'll never regret being with you, only the way I left you. I wasn't ready for a relationship, and what I felt with you scared the bejesus out of me. I walked. No, I ran, as fast and as far as I could. But you found me. And there was no way I could keep my hands off you. I needed you. And every time we were together, the need for you grew stronger and I ran faster in the other direction."

He moved inside her because he had to. Couldn't hold the need at bay any longer. "Then one night, the need overcame the fear, and, instead of coming to you, telling you what was going on in my head, I painted you. I didn't realize the secrets you held until I saw them in the painting. I was willing to ignore them, have you, no matter what you were hiding. Then I found out, and god, I lost it."

Flexing his hips, he pulled out then joined with her again, slowly filling her so both of them felt the connection being made. "I lashed out. Blamed you for everything wrong in my life, but you set me straight. I didn't see it at first, but when I did, I had to paint you again. Had to paint what I see when I look at you."

"What do you see?"

"Perfection. My heart." He pulled out once more and drove back in, more forceful this time. "I love you, MacKenzie Carlysle. I think I fell in love with you the minute you propositioned me at the airport bar."

Her eyes misted over. "Oh, Will. I fell in love with you when you asked me if I knew a place we could go. I needed to feel alive, to be desired. You gave me exactly what I asked for then broke my heart."

"I'm so sorry, Kenzie, baby." He retreated then advanced again. "I was in over my head in so many ways. I was afraid to stay. Afraid I'd follow you wherever you were going and I'd never find myself again."

"I guess it's lucky we were going to the same place."

"Fate."

This time, when he moved, she moved with him.

"I love you, MacKenzie."

"I love you, too."

About the Author

USA Today Best-Selling author Roz Lee is the author of twenty-five romances. The first, The Lust Boat, was born of an idea acquired while on a Caribbean cruise with her family and soon blossomed into a five book series published by Red Sage. Following her love of baseball, she turned her attention to sexy athletes in tight pants, writing the critically acclaimed Mustangs Baseball series.

Roz has been married to her best friend, and high school sweetheart, for nearly four decades. Roz and her husband have two grown daughters, a son-in-law, and are the proud grandparents to the cutest little boy ever.

Even though Roz has lived on both coasts, her heart lies in between, in Texas. A Texan by birth, she can trace her family back to the Republic of Texas. With roots that deep, she says, "You can't ever really leave."

When Roz isn't writing, she's reading, or traipsing around the country on one adventure or another. No trip is too small, no tourist trap too cheesy, and no road unworthy of travel.

Other Titles by Roz Lee

Mustangs Baseball Series
Inside Heat
Going Deep
Bases Loaded
Switch Hitter
Spring Training
Strike Out
Free Agent
Seasoned Veteran

Lone Star Honky-Tonk Short Story Series
Lookin' Good
Hung Up
Rockin' O
Barbed Wire
Saddle Up

Lesbian Office Romance Series
A Spanking Good Christmas
Special Delivery Valentine
Pushing the Envelope
Yours, Thankfully

Billionaire Brides Series
The Backdoor Billionaire's Bride
The Yankee Billionaire's Bride
The Reluctant Billionaire Bride

Lothario Series

The Lust Boat
Show Me the Ropes
Love Me Twice
Four of Hearts
Under the Covers
Also:
Lost Melody
Suspended Game
Sweet Carolina
Still Taking Chances
Banged on Broadway
The Middlethorpe Chronicles
Hearts on Fire
Summer Sizzle Anthology

Made in the USA
Columbia, SC
31 January 2020